"It's been a great Christmas," Oliver murmured

He rolled over in bed, his heated naked body pressing against Peggy's back, allowing him to enter her from behind.

"You feel so good," she whispered shakily, sighing as he drove inside.

She was wearing a Santa hat he'd picked up at the store earlier. "You've been naughty," he said hoarsely, reading the message scrawled in red on the white brim.

"Maybe I need a spanking," she teased.

Oliver eased away from her, loving how she gasped over each inch of his withdrawal. Slipping his palm downward, he gave her a love tap that drew a cry— not of pain, but of pleasure.

"Nice," she corrected cheekily, reaching up and turning the brim to the side that said, "I've been nice."

"If you've been nice," he teased, "then maybe Santa will give you something special for Christmas. What do you want?"

Her breath caught and she shifted her body. "This."

With a groan, Oliver rolled her over and entered her again with a long, deep satisfying thrust.

Merry Christmas...

Dear Reader,

Merry Christmas!

Manhattan at Christmastime has always been special. During the holidays, the city that never sleeps is charged with a giving spirit and the legendary heart for which New Yorkers have always been known.

I hope you'll join me this month in celebrating, and that you'll enjoy *The Sex Files*, where two strangers come together in the city both to solve a little mystery and fall in love while spending the holiday in some of the most pleasurable ways imaginable....

I do hope this story makes you smile. And don't forget to check out tryblaze.com!

Wishing the happiest holiday to you and yours,

Jule McBride

Books by Jule McBride

HARLEQUIN TEMPTATION

866—NAUGHTY BY NATURE
875—THE HOTSHOT*
883—THE SEDUCER*
891—THE PROTECTOR*

*Big Apple Bachelor miniseries

THE SEX FILES

Jule McBride

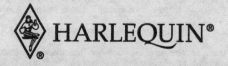

HARLEQUIN®

TORONTO • NEW YORK • LONDON
AMSTERDAM • PARIS • SYDNEY • HAMBURG
STOCKHOLM • ATHENS • TOKYO • MILAN • MADRID
PRAGUE • WARSAW • BUDAPEST • AUCKLAND

For Eileen Keator—
New Yorker, photographer, friend.
And best of all, a woman who dares
to be herself and enjoy life.
You go, girl!

ISBN 0-373-79071-6

THE SEX FILES

Copyright © 2002 by Julianne Moore.

This edition published by arrangement with Harlequin Books S.A.

® and TM are trademarks of the publisher. Trademarks indicated with ® are registered in the United States Patent and Trademark Office, the Canadian Trade Marks Office and in other countries.

Visit us at www.eHarlequin.com

Printed in U.S.A.

1

"WELL, KATE," Oliver Vargo was saying conversationally as he leaned forward in a white-upholstered sectional chair. "I can hardly take personal credit for bringing psychological talents to law enforcement. It's really nothing new."

"Please don't be modest, Mr. Vargo," replied Kate Olsen, the redheaded interviewer for NBC's *Rise and Shine* show and talking head for the evening news. She chuckled knowingly. "The psychological profiles you've produced for the FBI have led to the arrest of countless felons, including many who committed crimes previously deemed unsolvable."

"Psyching out the other guy is as old as crime itself," Oliver returned agreeably.

"Yet some experts devalue criminal profiling, saying it's not an exact science." Before he could respond, Kate turned toward the camera, beginning a slow segue toward the commercial break. "For anyone tuning in, our guest today is FBI agent Oliver Vargo, whose first book *How Evil Thinks* was one of the longest-running nonfiction bestsellers ever on the *New York Times* list." Leaning, Kate lifted a hardcover from a glass-topped coffee table and held it up, her manicured fingers bracketing Oliver's photograph.

"His latest book, *Catching Crooks the Old-Fashioned Way*, promises to be every bit as successful.

"In a moment, we'll need to pause for a commercial break," she continued, returning her gaze to Oliver, "but before we do, what can you tell us about your fascinating book?"

As a wry smile curled the corners of his mouth, his dark eyes twinkled in a way that wasn't lost on the camera. "In ten words or less?" he joked, playing the audience like a natural while clearly noticing a cue from someone off-camera, probably a producer.

"Don't worry," said Kate with an encouraging laugh. "We'll have time after our break, too!"

"My book defends criminal profiling," Oliver said, turning serious. "Something that—as you've pointed out, Kate—has been debunked by many as mumbo jumbo."

"Even though the methods are successful?"

"Yes." He continued in a deep voice that quickened with passion for his subject. "Detractors argue that profiling is a new method for solving crimes, but it's really more tried-and-true than scientific evidence we readily accept, such as fingerprinting, or analyzing hair and fiber samples."

"Fascinating," Kate murmured, her eyes intent. "For those who are just tuning in, what exactly *is* profiling?"

"Profiling is the old-fashioned way to solve crimes," explained Oliver.

"And what does it take to become a profiler?"

"Too much schooling," he joked. "Profilers have dual college degrees in law enforcement and psychology. Some, like me, go on to get post-graduate degrees. Technically, I'm a licensed psychologist.''

"Wow," she said.

"Yes," he agreed, "it is exciting. When we profile, we're playing armchair detective, much as Sherlock Holmes did. We'll slowly walk through a crime scene, pretending we're the criminal, to get into his or her mind—"

With every word, Oliver became more intense; dark eyebrows met, accentuating a high forehead from which black, wavy hair was slicked back. "We try to think as the criminal thinks. See as the criminal sees. Feel as the criminal feels.''

For once in *Rise and Shine*'s three-year run, Kate looked as if she hadn't heard a word her interview subject was saying. She looked mesmerized by Oliver's face. "There's something else our audience— and particularly *women*—want to know," she murmured when he was finished.

He blinked, as if talking about work had transported him to an alien planet and he was only now returning. "Yes?"

"We know you deal with the darker side of human nature, Mr. Vargo, but how about the lighter side?"

Now he looked uncertain. "Lighter side?"

Kate smiled indulgently. "Yes, lighter side. What do you do for fun?" When he still seemed mildly stupefied, she plunged on. "According to your biography, you're unmarried and based in Quantico, Virginia, near the FBI's profiling headquarters where you usually work."

"True, but I've been traveling this year, Kate, and

for the next six weeks, I'm assigned right here in New York City. I'll be here during Thanksgiving and Christmas.''

"As hard as you're working, and with so much travel, do you plan to take time off for the holidays?''

"Sure. Although my folks are leaving the country for Christmas, and my sister's going on vacation with a friend. I guess I'll…'' He looked stumped.

"You mean there's no special someone?''

DURING THE PAUSE that followed, the tall blonde who was watching the show resituated herself. Tucking a black nightie beneath her behind, she squirmed, grimacing at the discomfort of the thong she wore. Nestling against the satin headboard of a king-size bed at the Plaza Hotel, she groaned when the movements caused her breasts to spill from the scooped neckline, then she felt tears sting her eyes. She wished she could cry, but she hadn't since….

She pushed the thought away. One manicured thumb was on the remote control; the other tapped the cover of Oliver Vargo's new book. "Well, c'mon,'' she whispered, tossing her head to dislodge a lock of honey-streaked hair that fell over a brown eye, obscuring her vision. "Is there someone special?'' If Oliver had a lover it could interfere with her plans to contact him.

Kate Olsen turned to the camera again. "Sorry, but we'll have to wait until after the commercial break for the answer. So don't go away. When we come back, agent and author Oliver Vargo, tells us if his personal life's as adventurous as his professional one!''

Glancing down, the viewer surveyed his picture. ''I would recognize him from a million miles away,'' she murmured, sucking in a shaky breath. After all, she'd long been a fan of his work, and she'd been tailing him around Manhattan all afternoon, wondering how she should approach him.

She continued blinking, hoping her tears might start to fall but she was still in shock. Yesterday a bullet had almost claimed her life, and now she desperately needed Oliver Vargo's help. Already, she'd been having a rough day when, last night, she'd gone to the home of her fiancé—only to find him in bed with another woman, a woman she'd recognized from a wanted poster as a bank robber. As unbelievable as the events seemed, they'd really happened. The woman's name was Susan Jones. Even worse, the man in question, Miles McLaughlin, her fiancé, was an FBI agent.

''Incredible,'' she whispered now, perspiration beading on her upper lip.

As soon as she'd entered the bedroom, Susan Jones had rolled away from Miles—they'd been making love—grabbed his revolver from a bedside table and aimed at her heart. She'd frozen, standing there like a deer caught in headlights, wondering what her fiancé was doing in bed with this woman. Shock, betrayal and terror were rippling through her when she heard the distinctive sound of Susan's voice as she turned to Miles and said, ''What's *she* doing here?''

Then the bullet had exploded, splintering the wood

of the door frame near her head. She'd whirled in terror, hitting a hallway first, then a staircase. She was at the downstairs door when she heard the *pa-choo* of a second shot. She hadn't looked back. Her heart hammering, she'd kept running. And she'd been running ever since.

She'd been so shocked, so scared, that an hour had passed before she completely registered what she'd seen. It was astonishing enough that she'd seen an FBI agent in bed with a bank robber. Devastating, since she'd been engaged to him. But when she'd calmed down, she'd registered the open suitcase she'd seen shoved under the bed. Money had been stuffed into the case, no doubt from the bank heist for which Susan Jones was wanted. Was her fiancé—ex-fiancé—she mentally corrected—involved in the woman's crimes? And why hadn't she seen through him?

She hated men, she thought now, shivering. Yes, this betrayal was the last straw. A woman had nearly killed her, true. But ultimately, a man was responsible for what had happened—and she was going to make him pay. Oliver Vargo was the perfect man to cast in the role of Avenging Angel, too. Now she was glad to feel her eyes stinging again. She'd felt so stunned, she hadn't yet been able to have a real cry, and it was yesterday that the shots had been fired. Right now, yesterday felt like a century ago.

Despite her terror, every time she looked at Oliver Vargo, something inside her melted and she wanted to reconsider her vendetta against men. She shivered again. If not for her profession, none of this would have happened. Hadn't her mother been devastated, saying what she did for a living was too dangerous? But who could have foreseen that she'd meet a crooked FBI agent while she was working?

"I've got to find someplace safe to go when I check out," she murmured.

But where? It would be hours until Oliver Vargo got off work and she could approach him for help. She didn't have time to dress and try to catch him leaving the TV studio. She wasn't sure she trusted him, but she did need help from a smart FBI insider who knew how to use a gun and who wouldn't mind protecting a woman. And Oliver looked honest, though appearances could lie. Still, because she knew his work, and because Miles was an agent, she felt safer going to Oliver Vargo than to the police...

Opening the cover of his book, she skimmed the bio, noting his degrees in law enforcement and psychology, an explosive ten-year career and the long list of criminals he'd caught. He was unmarried and lived alone, just as Kate Olsen had said, but the picture showed him lying in a hammock in front of a family-size home. He was reading a book.

"The New York Public library," she whispered, feeling a jolt of relief at the idea. When she left the Plaza, she'd lose herself in the crowds at the library, read Oliver's book, and then go to Grand Central Station. The Forty-second Street entrance was across from the midtown FBI office where Oliver worked, and she could leave the duffel in one of the train station's lockers. She'd have to be careful, of course.

But at five o'clock, when Oliver left work, she'd find out where he was staying and approach him.

"And we're back from commercial break!" Kate Olsen's voice interrupted her thoughts. "We're here with FBI agent, Oliver Vargo, the bestselling author of *How Evil Thinks* and *Catching Crooks the Old-Fashioned Way.* "Well, Oliver," continued Kate. "We know you've been touring the country, training other FBI agents to profile criminals as well as promoting your new book. But why are you in New York?"

"To help work out kinks in the bureau's new, state-of-the-art computer software," he explained.

"Could you tell us more?"

"Sure. Our new computer software is called Quick Composite. As I mentioned, profilers assemble facts about possible suspects, imagining how the criminal thinks and feels. Now, with Quick Composite, the FBI will be able to input that information into computers and generate pictures of suspects."

"Pictures?"

He nodded. "Very similar to photographs. We'll know what the criminal might look like when we find him. Or her. As we work, we deduce facts about the suspect—such as gender and race. Height and weight. Hair and eye color. Now, as we input those facts into Quick Composite, a computer will produce a picture."

"Like a police artist's sketch?"

"Exactly, Kate. Except this is more sophisticated. The image is more accurate and of photographic quality."

"Amazing," said Kate dreamily, as if captivated. "Do you really think a picture of a suspect—one generated by inputting facts about a crime—might be identical to that of a real criminal when you catch him?"

"Or her," Oliver added. "And yes. Absolutely. Our computer-generated pictures should resemble the mug shots when we arrest criminals. It sounds amazing, but new technology is emerging all the time."

Kate's eyebrows knitted. "But how does using new technology fit with your desire to solve crimes the old-fashioned way?"

He chuckled, as if to say she had a point. "It doesn't, Kate. I'm of the old school. And I'm here in New York to play devil's advocate with the team creating the Quick Composite software. My job's to point out whatever the new technology misses."

"And then?"

He sounded relieved. "I'm going home to Quantico."

"Where your personal life is as intriguing as your professional one?"

Oliver shook his head. "Believe me," he joked, "I get enough excitement at the office. It's my younger sister, Anna, whose personal life sizzles. She lives here in New York City, and she's a statistician for…" He paused to build anticipation. "The Sex Files."

"The Sex Files?" the viewer whispered.

The annual report of fun statistics about North Americans' erotic behavior was being advertised all over Manhattan—on the sides of city buses and in the subway. Scheduled for its usual Christmas release, the magazine-style booklet was fashioned to look like a red-and-green file folder and was the perfect stocking stuffer.

"Can you give our audience a sneak preview?" urged Kate.

"It's top secret. I can only say that this is the best Sex Files yet, and you should plan to race out and get your copy."

As she watched him plug his little sister's work instead of his own, the viewer's heart missed a beat. "Family values," she whispered. "A good sign." He might be work obsessed, but he seemed to possess integrity.

"Well," said Kate, wrapping up, "next time you join us on *Rise and Shine,* I want you to do us a big favor."

"Anything for you, Kate."

Kate grinned. "I want you to take the statistics from the Sex Files—all the facts about the most erotic behaviors in North America—and run the information through the FBI's new Quick Composite software."

Catching her drift, Oliver chuckled. "I see. You want me to generate photographs, showing what the sexiest man and woman would look like—if they existed?" Before Kate could respond, he continued. "I'll be glad to, Kate, but before saying goodbye to our audience, I'd like to add that I usually find women the way I solve crimes."

When Oliver Vargo looked into the camera, the blond woman shivered again, and for the first time since last night, it wasn't from fear, but from the man's dark, penetrating gaze. Her belly clenched and her body tingled. "I'd love to see the effect you have on women in real life," she whispered. Even though he was on TV, her erogenous zones ached. If only her reaction to him could be as simple as raw lust…

For a second, she indulged the feeling, forgetting her troubles. No one had tried to kill her. She could go home and to work and use her bank and credit cards. She was wearing clothes that fit, too. Clothes she now imagined Oliver Vargo removing….

"I find women the way I solve crimes," he repeated, then added, "the old-fashioned way."

Did he mean he enjoyed missionary-style sex? Or taking a woman from behind? Or just cuddling, holding hands and kissing?

She shook her head to clear the thoughts. No doubt anything sexual with the man would be great, but at the moment, she had other needs. Even if she didn't totally trust him, she was going to have to ask for his help.

"OH, C'MON, Big Brother," Anna Vargo begged the next day at noon, seating herself on Oliver's desk and digging a hand into an Au Bon Pain bag, pulling out two sandwiches. "Kate Olsen's idea was inspired! All I want you to do is run the Sex Files statistics through your Quick Composite software."

Oliver groaned, staring at the computer screen, which was running a list of the country's most wanted criminals. "I'm working."

"Be a sport," she coaxed, unperturbed by his lack of immediate compliance. "I brought ham and Gouda on rye with hot mustard." She waggled the sandwich in front of him. "Your favorite. And a double mocha-ccino. Besides, if you don't help me, I'll call Mom and Dad and tattle."

"They're in Utah. Besides, bribery's illegal," he retorted, taking the sandwich and unwrapping it. "You seem to forget you're talking to an FBI agent."

"Yeah, right. One I've seen in house slippers."

As he bit into the sandwich, she flashed a smile, her teeth as straight and white as her brother's. She had his black, wavy hair, too, although she dressed more stylishly, wearing trendy, thick-framed, black glasses and a tailored, front-zippered black leather jacket with black jeans. Oliver was wearing wide-waled corduroys and a white shirt.

He said, "I don't own house slippers, Anna."

"I was speaking metaphorically," she quipped, taking a healthy bite of her own sandwich and wash-ing it down with a gulp of latte. "That's the problem with law enforcers, you know," she chided. "You have no imagination. You're too literal."

"We have imaginations," Oliver countered, pre-tending to be wounded even though his dark eyes were sparkling.

"Oh, really?" Anna didn't look convinced as she glanced through a glassed-in window of her brother's office at a sea of open-concept cubicles. "Gray was an inspired choice. All you G-men are regular Martha Stewarts."

"My office in Quantico is colorful," Oliver de-fended. "This space is only temporary, Anna."

"Okay," she conceded. "But everybody else, be-sides you, has a gray cubicle. Which only goes to show that you don't fit in, Big Brother. Face it, you're a renegade. A rebel.'' Her voice was rising. "A man who'll—''

"Run your Sex Files through my Quick Composite software?''

"It'll only take a minute, Ollie,'' she urged, polishing off the first half of her sandwich and reaching for the rest. "Everybody at the office wants to know what North America's most erotic guy looks like. And you're the only one who can show us.''

Grinning, he opened his arms wide.

She rolled her eyes. "You? Oh, please.'' Reaching into the pocket of her leather jacket, she pulled out a CD. "Here. Just stick this in your ROM.''

As if he could deny Anna anything. She was the only woman on earth who could get away with calling him Ollie. "That's the new Sex Files?'' Oliver queried, pretending to hedge as he continued eating, but only because he loved teasing her. "You're going to get me fired, you know.''

"Never.'' She smirked. "You're too good at your job.''

"Pride goeth before a fall.''

"Oh, don't get puritanical.'' She groaned. "From the way those sparks were flying on *Rise and Shine,* I—and everybody else—was imagining how you and Kate Olsen must have gone at it after you finished taping that show yesterday.''

"Did not,'' he said.

Not that Kate Olsen hadn't tried. Practically salivating, she'd come into the dressing room without knocking, and when she'd found he was only changing shirts, not pants, she'd looked seriously disappointed. She'd propositioned him, too. Reaching over and cupping his privates was about as direct as it could get.

Why he hadn't gone for it, Oliver couldn't say. But ever since he'd finished building his dream home near Quantico, women hadn't held the same appeal. He figured it was because he was starting to look for something more than just sex. For somebody who intrigued him enough to share a life with. Or maybe, perish the thought, he'd just been too damn tired.

Between giving workshops on profiling, traveling to scenes of unsolved crimes around the country and promoting the new book, he'd been in fifty cities in the past twenty-five days. He'd lived in a string of hotels he didn't even want to contemplate, and now he was having trouble sleeping in New York because of the noise.

At least Anna was leaving tomorrow. He loved his sister, and was sorry they wouldn't be able to visit during most of his stay, but it wasn't as if she didn't visit Quantico on weekends. His New York assignment had unfortunately coincided with a vacation she'd planned with her boyfriend, Vic, a photographer for the Sex Files. Since this year's Sex Files had been put to bed, the two had angled for—and gotten—a six-week unpaid leave. After they left for the Virgin Islands, Oliver could move from his hotel into their tiny—but quiet—West Village apartment.

And then he could finally sleep, providing their wily black cat, Midnight, let him. At least there'd be no more wake-up calls, intrusive maids and newspapers shoved under his door. Glancing around the office, Oliver decided the only thing worse than hotels was the new paperless FBI.

Like every large company, the FBI was deciding that hard-copy records took up too much space. Data was being transferred to computers, then destroyed. Trouble was, there was a huge margin for error in relying on electronic information. When Oliver's e-ticket from L.A. to New York wasn't at the airport, for example, Oliver had to buy another ticket that cost the agency—and ultimately the taxpayer—twice the price of the initial ticket.

The flight was a nightmare, too. Every time Oliver boarded an airplane, the seats got smaller and the food tasted more like plastic. How flight attendants survived, he'd never know. He sighed, thinking of the wanted posters usually displayed in airports and post offices. This week they were being recalled, soon to be replaced by an easier-to-read format. If you asked Oliver, it was all busywork, generated by people who weren't good enough agents to actually solve crimes.

"You still here, Oliver?" Before he could respond, Anna added, "You know that all work and no play makes Jack a dull boy, right?"

"Good thing my name's not Jack."

She nodded at a blond man in an expensive suit wending his way through the cubicles. A distinctive birthmark stained his left cheek. "That's Miles McLaughlin, right? He looks like Don Johnson on the *Miami Vice* reruns." She paused. "And you're right. He also looks like a jerk."

Oliver eyed the head of the Information Systems

Department, brainchild for the paperless FBI and co-creator of the new Quick Composite software. "What tipped you off? That he's wearing sunglasses inside the building?"

Anna laughed, contemplating a tall, massively built black man with a shaved head who was as nattily dressed as Miles. "Yep. His sidekick looks like an African-American Bruce Willis."

"Kevin Hall." He was the other half of the Quick Composite team. "In their honor, I'm calling my next book *Disappearing Evidence*. Or maybe the *Virtual FBI*..."

"What about *FBI Dot-Com*?"

"Clever. They're referring to this place as the E-Bureau."

Anna giggled. "Really?"

"Really."

"You sound cynical. I thought you backed the bureau all the way."

Oliver had done so publicly, but for every criminal caught by new methods, others roamed free and, as far as he was concerned, the agency's E-Bureau was siphoning manpower. Destroying hard-copy records was crazy. "You should see what's happening downstairs."

"That bad, huh?"

The basement was in pandemonium. On the first floor, files from open cardboard boxes were being scanned into a central database. Upstairs, Miles and Kevin were holding meetings, announcing that in the new global economy, evidence was going to become superfluous. "J. Edgar Hoover's probably rolling over in his grave,'' Oliver muttered. He slugged back a last gulp of mochaccino just as lightning flashed, illuminating the entrance to Grand Central Station.

"Big Brother,'' Anna said, shaking her head, "you look grim. I think Kate Olsen hit the nail on the head.'' Laughing, her eyes twinkling, Anna reiterated Kate's words. "'We know you deal with the darker side of life, Mr. Vargo, but what about the lighter side?''' Pausing, Anna offered her best dumb-doofus expression, then lightly mocked her brother, saying, "Duh? Lighter side? Fun? What's that?''

Oliver couldn't help but smile.

"Which brings me to something else,'' she plunged on. "While I'm in the Virgin Islands, promise me you'll meet some people. I'm leaving phone numbers for all my girlfriends who developed crushes on you when they saw you on TV. They all want you in the worst way.''

"So, it was you who put all those condoms in my wallet.''

"Who did you think it was? The condom fairy?'' He chuckled as she continued. "You seem stressed and overtired, and you look like you need a vacation. Since it's been so long that you've obviously forgotten, sex is the closest thing to a vacation when you don't have time to go out of town.''

"It hasn't been *that* long.''

She leveled him with a stare. "Did you do it with Kate Olsen?''

"None of your business.''

"I didn't think so,'' Anna returned.

Damn. His little sister had been playing matchmaker ever since his arrival. When it came to fixing him up, he was beginning to think there was nothing she wouldn't try. While he considered calling one of her friends for a date, he looked down at the entrance to Grand Central and a sidewalk teeming with open umbrellas. People without them crowded under awnings, craning their necks to stare at the downpour as if they expected the rain to stop sometime soon. Others lifted coats over their heads and ran through the deluge.

"Have fun while I'm gone," Anna was saying. "You work all the time, Ollie."

So did she, and the way Oliver figured it, they were lucky to love their work. Anna's boyfriend, Vic, was just as passionate and could talk for hours about the various ways photographers manipulated images. Kate Olsen also enjoyed working, so it was too bad she hadn't rung his chimes. The truth was, lately he'd been rejecting most women. It was as if, deep down, he'd decided on an image of what he was really looking for and now he was waiting for that dream woman to materialize.

"I've changed my mind," Anna announced, drawing Oliver from his reverie as she put the Sex Files CD into his ROM drive. "We'll get a picture of the sexiest woman first. That'll get your juices flowing, so you'll be ready to call all my friends who are dying to meet you."

This was definitely more intriguing than getting a printout of the sexiest man. "I'm working on the Most Wanted List."

Anna leaned and jiggled the mouse, moving the cursor. "We can keep that program open," she assured. "We'll minimize it and work in another window." He watched as she hit RUN.

They waited.

And then text filled the screen. Anna groaned in disappointment. "I thought you said we'd get a picture."

"We will when you scroll down."

"Oh, but this is good," she whispered, reading the words. "America's Sexiest Woman would be named Cameron," she announced breathlessly.

"And according to this, she'd be tall," he added. "Five-eleven."

"Her measurements are thirty-six, twenty-four, thirty-six," continued Anna. "And she loves wearing sexy clothes."

"She sounds like a walking cliché." Still, as he continued reading, there was no denying the pull of arousal. Barely suppressing a shiver, he tried to ignore the tightening below his belt, but it only increased when he read that Cameron never wore panties under her Lycra slacks, body-hugging knit dresses and silk teddies.

When she has to get dressed at all, the text read, *Cameron likes to get out and have spicy, erotic adventures. She especially loves the excitement of world travel and meeting new male playmates. She likes a hint of danger, too. Exploring kinky aphrodisiacs is her favorite pastime, and she dabbles in everything from body paints to edible undies. Cameron will do absolutely anything—and everything—to please her man.*

Oliver was surprised by how easily he was getting sucked into the fantasy. He prided himself on not being sexist and for liking a woman for her mind, though he thoroughly enjoyed the rest. "If I was a woman," he commented, dragging a hand through his hair, "I'd hate this kind of thing."

Anna laughed. "But you're a man."

As such, he had to admit that he found this fantasy woman appealing. "Point taken."

Anna merely shrugged. "Ah. You don't scroll. There's a link." She clicked on the mouse. In the instant before the image of America's Sexiest Woman filled the screen, she said, "So, this is what Cameron would look like if she were real."

Oliver felt as if somebody had punched him. Her hair was dark blond, a shade most would call honey, but it was shot through with everything from pale straw to bumblebee yellow to strands of brilliant white. Looking as soft as silk, it hung in loose waves past her shoulders, tightening into curls where the ends rested on a tan cashmere sweater.

His eyes dropped to her breasts. Slightly aroused nipples pebbled under the shirt. In contrast to what he'd felt with Kate Olsen, he found himself imagining cupping those mounds, then slowly stroking their creamy sides and swirling his tongue around their excited, satiny tips. When his eyes traveled toward her face, he couldn't tear them away. Her neck was so nice. Very round, very creamy. And her face… "She reminds me of film stars from the forties."

"Veronica Lake, maybe," Anna agreed.

Parted in a jagged line, her hair framed her face, waving over one of her unusually wide-set dark eyes, lending an air of mystery. Miles McLaughlin hadn't been kidding about the photographic quality of the pictures generated by Quick Composite, either. Cameron definitely looked real.

And familiar.

He could swear he'd seen her somewhere, but that was probably because she was such a cliché-woman, blond and dark-eyed with a perfect body. Because the picture looked so real, he had to remind himself that she didn't really exist as he continued surveying her.

Her face was closer to round than oval; her cheekbones high and slanted. Light-brown eyebrows arched on poreless, pink-toned skin. Her mouth was decidedly kissable, the red, glistening lips parted slightly. The velvet tip of a tongue was exposed, touching a very slight, sexy gap between her two front teeth.

"Before you get carried away, Oliver," murmured Anna, studying his expression, "please remember she's not real."

He barely heard.

"I'll come back when you're not so bedazzled," she continued on a sigh, planting a kiss on her brother's cheek. "I still want to see the sexiest guy. But now I'm late. I've got to run to Bloomie's for another bathing suit to take to the islands. See you for dinner? After work, Vic and I want to take you to Little Italy. We want you to meet a friend of ours. If you hit it off, you can spend time together on Thanksgiving or Christmas. Her family—"

"Is going out of town, just like you and Vic, and Mom and Dad. C'mon, quit worrying about me. I'll be fine over the holidays. And I'll get my own dates."

"When?"

He merely shrugged, his gaze returning to the computer screen. When he looked up again, Anna was gone. Because he turned instinctively toward the window to catch a glimpse of her, he was staring down at Forty-second Street when lightning jagged across the sky, illuminating the entrance to Grand Central Station.

The flash lasted only a heartbeat, just long enough for his jaw to slacken and for his heart to miss a beat as the angry sky turned dark again. He felt sure he was going crazy. But she'd been standing there, hadn't she? He shook his head in disbelief, but he could swear he'd seen the same woman whose image still filled his computer screen.

"Cameron," he murmured. But it was impossible. It wasn't really her. It couldn't be.

No. The lightning had come as fast as a camera flash. Oliver was far away, too. And besides, Cameron wasn't even real. She was just a computer-generated image they'd gotten by crossing the Sex Files with Quick Composite.

And yet he could swear he'd seen her standing under an awning, staring up at him. She was exactly the same as the picture in every detail, tall and curvy with blond hair that fell over one eye. She'd been wearing a green raincoat. His mouth went dry as he edged closer to the window. Not a man usually given to flights of fancy, he set his mouth in a grim line as he stared down, his eyes piercing the rain and darkness.

When the lightning flashed again, the woman was gone.

2

"WHY, YOU KNOW I'll do absolutely anything—and everything—to please a man, Oliver," Cameron was murmuring huskily a few nights later. As Oliver dreamily splayed his hands on the warm mattress and buried his face in a down pillow, she continued. "I live to make a man happy! Exploring kinky aphrodisiacs is my favorite pastime. I'm the kind of woman who lives only to titillate, and tonight I've decided you're the special man who's going to be my bed partner. Hmm...isn't this exciting? Doesn't this feel good, Oliver?"

Clad in only a black silk teddy, Cameron was purring into his ear as she ran a rose-red nail down his chest, tickling the unruly black hairs that bisected his muscular pectorals before slowly tracing each nipple. As she brought him ever closer to the brink, his eyes roved hungrily over her. Her breasts were creamy and spilling from the low-cut garment, but unfortunately not enough that he could catch more than a glimpse of her tight, straining nipples, something that made him groan. Heat pooled in his belly when he took in the teddy's hem, which hit where her shapely thighs met. And when she moved, he could see matching panties that covered just enough to hint at the hidden temptations she had in store for him.

"Are you enjoying this, Oliver?" she coaxed, dampening a finger with her tongue before continuing her exploration of his chest in a way that made him shiver. "What about this, Oliver?" she queried, using both hands to massage his pectorals. Inching down, her thumbs dipped into crevices as she explored his rib cage. "Or this?"

"It all feels great," he managed hoarsely. "Just great, Cameron." He'd had sex with a lot of women, and he'd fallen in love with some, but he'd never experienced anything like this. Cameron was wrapping him around her little finger.

Pulling in her scent, he awaited more maddening teasing as Cameron's hands traveled farther southward, her usually soulful brown eyes turning wicked with sensual intent as she paused to swirl mindshattering patterns on his lower belly, leaving his skin awash with ripples of tingling warmth.

Tensing expectantly, his backside tightened; as pressure built in his loins, he let her do whatever she wanted, silently begging for mercy when she used the backs of her hands to stroke his upper thighs. Every inch of him felt prickly as her now-splayed fingers came closer to the wild tangle of his pubic hair. He arched as she twined her fingers in it, but she still wasn't touching where he most wanted...

Suddenly, she stopped and merely traced lazy circles around his navel as if she was bored out of her mind. "Cameron," Oliver warned, his eyes raking *down her body, his distracted mind becoming hazier with need as she tortured him.*

"What?" she asked innocently.

Shutting his eyes in frustration, he dragged a hand into her hair and closed his fist, lightly tugging. "C'mon, Cameron. Quit fooling around. Touch me."

"I am touching you, silly."

"You know what I mean."

He was throbbing, wanting her so much it hurt, and if she didn't caress him more intimately, he'd die from the need. Why wasn't the woman doing something more? Hadn't she said pleasing men was her sole reason for living? She'd said it in that encouraging voice he couldn't resist, too. "I thought you were America's sexiest woman," he challenged.

"I am," she purred. "That's why you're feeling so…" She whisked a finger around his navel again.

"Frustrated?" he supplied. Yes, he definitely preferred more cerebral women. Of course he did. And yet every time Cameron insisted their relationship be focused on pure pleasure, she left him no choice but to respond. Sex was all this woman wanted….

Cameron was smiling at him mysteriously, looking just like the Mona Lisa *as she continued drawing mindless designs on his sensitized skin. He uttered a strangled sound as she reached between her own legs, cupping herself. "Say pretty please, Oliver," she whispered, a wavy lock of hair falling over her left eye.*

"Pretty please," Oliver murmured, his voice gruff, his pulse quickening as he played along, knowing

he'd be happy to indulge in any game this woman initiated... "Tease," he accused.

"You love it."

He smiled, looking down into the gaping neckline of the teddy, able to see perky nipples. "Yeah," he said. "I do."

"Is this all a big boy like you wants, Oliver?" she taunted. "Wouldn't you rather feel something more substantial on all your hot, quivering skin? Wouldn't you rather feel my mouth?"

As he twisted on the heated water bed his sister usually shared with her boyfriend, Oliver's eyes remained shut in sleep although his body was radiating with damp, feverish desire. Every time he tossed and turned, hoping to end the frustration of this dream, his movements displaced water. Warm waves rolled back, further exciting him by massaging his pelvis, and as he got even hotter, he thought of wet, cool things such as Cameron's mouth.

"Oh, Oliver—" Cameron was chuckling naughtily. "Maybe you'd like to model a pair of edible briefs for me. I know you read about how much I like them in the Sex Files. I bet you wish you could feel the languishing lap of my tongue as I lick off all your clothes...?"

He wasn't wearing any clothes in his dream, but Oliver didn't bother to correct her, not when she was whispering to him in that sweet voice, her breath fanning his ear in a way that made his lower body surge.

"Edible briefs?" *he whispered, hoping she'd say more. He'd heard of the novelty item, of course. Who hadn't? But he'd never felt the need to bring props into a bedroom. He loved women, and he enjoyed binding them to him using only his body, just the way he planned to do with Cameron.*

"Oh." She panted, her hand dropping another fraction. "Ah," she added as she scooted downward, settling between his legs, her eager eyes fixing where he'd gotten so hard. Reaching, she grasped the hem of the nightie and, as she lifted it over her head, he ceased to breathe. Lightly licking his lips, he took in her breasts...then the inward curve of her waist...then hips that flared down to...

After he eyed her panties—a scrap of black held together by two tiny red side bows—his hands reached up, brushing the erect tips of her breasts. "You have no idea what I'm going to do to you, Cameron," he warned, imagining tugging those bows with his teeth...

"Why don't you tell me? We've got all night." Before he could, she raggedly whispered, "Yes," her hands bracing against his thighs, her breasts thrusting for his caresses. She threw back her head, her pleasure building, her fingers squeezing into his thighs, the sight of her red fingernails against his skin sending another rush of heat through his veins.

His chest was tight now. Strong bands were wrapping around his ribs. Her hands had turned gentler, and they were rising on his legs like a river about to flood, moving higher...and higher...and higher...

When they bracketed his erection, his eyes settled on her inviting mouth. "Kiss me, Cameron," he commanded hoarsely, threading his hands deep into hair that felt like corn silk. Strands spilled through his fingers and curled against his wrist, most the color of whiskey in candlelight, the others shot through with different shades of blond. Dragging his nails across her scalp seemed to drive her wild. Good, he thought. Because he wanted her wild and abandoning herself to pleasure.

Her breath caught. "Where exactly do you want me to kiss you, Oliver?"

His voice lowered. "You know where."

"I have something else in mind."

She was making him writhe with annoyance! "What?"

Instead of doing him the courtesy of answering, she hopped from the bed, and as she reached for the bedside table, Oliver's whole world seemed to stop. A thong left her backside bare. Before he could react, she whirled, a bottle of mint-scented oil in her hand, and he watched, fascinated, as she squirted some into her hand. His mouth slackened as she set aside the bottle and massaged her own breasts, pressing them together, deepening the cleavage, and then slathering on the oil until the tips glistened and she was begging for relief that only he could give.

"Oh, yeah," he whispered as she lowered her chest toward his thighs, her lips only inches from his aroused flesh, her breath warm on his erection, her slender fingers feeling like heaven as they circled where he'd gone so taut. When she squeezed, his head reared back, the pressure more than he could stand, and when he felt her blond hair sweeping his thighs, the sensation added to his delight—and torture. The

*water bed churned as she kneeled astride, urging him
between her luscious, waiting breasts.*

*Thrusting into the slippery cleavage, he gasped.
The oil was mentholated, and with every mind-
bending movement, it warmed him and made him tin-
gle. Now he was so unbelievably hot...the oil was
frothing...the essence of mint was mixing with Cameron's heady musk. He was going to come. The cool
autumn-night air was bursting with scents, just as Oliver was about to burst...*

Vaguely, he realized a siren had sounded.

It came from far off, edging into his consciousness
at first, then becoming deafening as an ambulance or
police car passed beneath the window overlooking
Barrow Street. Blinking, he opened his eyes and sat
up in bed, his head pounding from the sudden movement. Whatever he'd been dreaming must have taken
him to the outer reaches of REM-phase sleep, because
he felt completely groggy.

Dragging a hand through his hair, he realized the
strands were damp with perspiration. And that he
wasn't in his own bed in Quantico. Nor was he in a
hotel.

"Anna's," he whispered, feeling mildly disoriented and surprised to find that his mouth was bone
dry. He'd kicked away most of the covers, and the
remaining sheet was twisted around his legs.

He was as hard as steel, too.

A groan rumbled in his chest as the dream came
back to him: Cameron's red nails tracing patterns on
his skin...the soft stir of her warm, panting
breath...the searing feeling as he'd slipped inside her

cleavage. Realizing he was still hovering on the brink of release, he drew a sharp breath, his eyes adjusting to the room's darkness. "Some dream," he murmured.

It wasn't the first time the nonexistent woman had entered his nocturnal world, teasing him to distraction. As he'd awakened, he was actually feeling that he couldn't live without her. Heaven help the woman if he ever really met her...

But of course that was crazy. She wasn't even real. She didn't even exist. "I feel like I'm losing my mind," Oliver whispered.

It had all started when Anna insisted on running the Sex Files statistics through the Quick Composite software, generating the picture of "Cameron." Ever since, the fantasy woman had been wreaking havoc in Oliver's life. On two occasions, he'd been convinced he'd actually seen her.

It was impossible, of course. Computer-generated women didn't materialize. But after Anna left his office, a woman who looked exactly like Cameron had been standing in the street outside Grand Central Station. He could swear to it. She'd been looking at him wistfully, as if she'd desperately wanted to approach him.

And then yesterday at five o'clock, when Oliver left his office, he'd been sure someone was following him. That, of course, *was* possible. He was a well-known FBI agent and author, and he'd been approached by fans often. Criminals, too.

As he'd been swept along by the rush-hour crowd on Forty-second Street, he'd glanced around, but it was raining hard and he didn't see anyone suspicious. After he'd ducked into a subway entrance, then transferred at Times Square to another train, he figured he'd lost the person.

But then, at the West Fourth Street station near Anna's apartment, he'd seen Cameron across the platform. Two train tracks separated them—one going uptown, one downtown—and a train was passing on Oliver's side; through the windows, he could see her in bits and snatches.

Astonished, he'd felt as if someone had breathed life into Cameron's computer-screen image again. But how? What was going on?

He'd taken in her tall figure, the wavy blond hair falling over her left eye and the green raincoat she wore over a black knit dress. Before he'd been aware he'd moved, he'd given chase. He'd grown up in Manhattan, and even after he'd moved to the D.C. area and his parents retired in Utah, he'd continued visiting because Anna was here, so he knew the subways like the back of his hand.

He'd jogged upstairs, passing turnstiles as he headed for the uptown platform, but just as he'd reached it, another train pulled in. The electronic doors opened, and he'd cursed inwardly as people spilled out of cars, then back inside. He'd reached the doors just as they glided shut. Cameron had been right on the other side of the glass! Her brown eyes had widened, and she'd swung her head, so hair fell across her face as if to disguise herself. She'd tried to back away, but she'd been hemmed in by other passengers.

Futilely, Oliver had lifted a hand as the train pulled away, as if to wave goodbye.

Now he shook his head to clear it of confusion. None of this made sense. He was haunted by a woman who didn't even exist. As a psychologist, he knew the mind could play tricks, so his best guess was that Anna was right. He was overworked and lonely, a state that had made him ripe for suggestion when he'd seen the image of "Cameron."

Besides, what man wouldn't fantasize about America's most erotic woman? Yeah, this was definitely a case of wishful thinking. That, or his subconscious was trying to tell him something. "Yeah," he whispered hoarsely, his body still aching with need. "That you need a woman." A *real* woman.

Memories of the X-rated dream came back, and he couldn't believe what lurked in his subconscious. He wasn't really sexist, and he dated smart, levelheaded professional women, not stacked blondes who painted their nails come-love-me red and whispered to him as if he'd just called a 1-900 number. "Edible briefs," he whispered, rubbing sleep from his eyes. Wow.

"Why don't you settle down, Midnight?" he added as Anna's black cat scampered along the windowsill, drawing back the curtain. As light shined into the bedroom, another siren sounded, and Oliver glanced at the digital bedside clock: *2:00 a.m.* So much for peace and quiet. During the day, when he'd visited Anna, this neighborhood had been deserted, but sometimes at night it was a different story.

Rising, he moved to the third-floor window, but instead of closing the curtain, Oliver stared through the rain into Nite-Lite, a club across the street. Usually the club's curtains were closed, but tonight, black-light strobes illuminated a packed dance floor. Everybody was gearing up for the holidays. It was depressing. Despite what he'd been saying to the contrary, Oliver wasn't thrilled about spending Christmas alone.

Usually he and Anna went to his folks' place in Utah. He felt a sudden, uncharacteristic tug at his heart when an image of the white farmhouse flashed in his mind. He could see the candles his mother put along the front walkway, as well as the wreath on the front door that Anna had made years ago in a crafts class. The tree, always cut by him and his father, was visible through the windows. This year, he'd miss taking long walks with Anna through the snow-dusted streets of the rural countryside....

Suddenly, Oliver leaned forward. "No," he muttered. "This is crazy!" He'd seen her again! Cameron had been at the window, wearing that same green raincoat. When the lights strobed off, she vanished. "A trick of the night," he whispered without any real conviction. He was a logical man. Computer-generated images didn't come to life. But it had looked so much like the woman on his computer....

Rain was mixing with exhaust fumes and smoke rising from subway grates. Everything looked eerie. Smoky. Besides, it was the time of year for phantoms—Halloween had just passed. Winter was almost here. Nevertheless, he considered getting dressed and going to the club to hunt for her. She didn't exist, though. Right? Between being on the road for a year and doing the promotion for his book, he was simply stressed, and he had every reason to be. With his upcoming time off during the holidays, he'd do himself a favor and take it easy.

Closing the curtain, he climbed into bed again, uttering a frustrated grunt when the water surged beneath him. Who had he seen in the window? he wondered as he drifted.

"Here…let me help you, Oliver." Her breath was closer now, so near that he caught whiffs of peppermint. At first, he thought it was toothpaste, then a breath mint—and then Oliver remembered the mentholated massage oil. Burying his face in a pillow, he realized the soft cushions were really Cameron's breasts…

"You don't mind if I lie beside you, do you, Oliver?" she was whispering.

"Be my guest, Cameron."

Naked, she glided a thigh over his hip. He was throbbing as he slid a hand between their bodies, gently guiding himself inside her slick, wet heat. Moments ago, he'd been ready to explode, and now, once more, with her hands reaching between them to stroke him, he was teetering on the brink.

He gasped as her hips rocked. She whispered, "Take me deeper, Oliver. Deeper. All the way." He lost control then. Suddenly, his mouth was everywhere. It closed possessively over her lips, and after he'd plundered her mouth, he dripped liquid kisses down the length of her neck until he went low enough to lather her breasts, lightly scraping his teeth against the puckered tips—gently biting, urgently coaxing.

She arched and panted, begging him, "Love me, Oliver. Oh, please love me. You're so hot. I can't get enough of you."

He couldn't get enough of Cameron, either. Flames seemed to lick inside his limbs, and the wild need for her was spinning inside him like a dancer. He danced along with her, his mind turning somersaults, then fading to black as he thrust harder, quicker, deeper. He was so close, almost there...

He was fast sleep when he came.

3

"WHERE ARE YOU?" Peggy Fox whispered, hugging her green raincoat to her waist to stay warm and nervously pushing away the strands of blond hair falling over her eye. How could she have lost Oliver in the crowd? Just a second ago, he'd been standing across Sixth Avenue, watching the Thanksgiving Day parade.

Now he was gone. She shuddered, either because of the chill air and fog, or because she couldn't decide whether or not to approach him. As soon as she'd left the Plaza Hotel, things had taken a turn for the worse. She'd found where Oliver was staying, all right—a downtown apartment on Barrow Street that belonged to the sister he'd mentioned on TV—but before she could solicit his help, one of the men he worked with had chased her through the subway. He was a tall, bald, massively built black man who bore a striking resemblance to Bruce Willis.

"Halt!" he'd yelled. "I'm Kevin Hall. FBI. You're wanted for questioning."

She'd bolted, somehow losing him. But why was an agent chasing her? And why would she be wanted for questioning? She hadn't done anything wrong. If

Kevin Hall thought she was guilty of something, did Oliver Vargo think the same?

He, too, had spotted her in the subway, in the West Fourth Street station, and he'd given chase, although unlike Agent Hall, he hadn't looked as if he wanted to arrest her. She'd had the distinct impression Oliver had realized she was following him, but until she knew for certain what was going on, she meant to play her cards close to the vest. Which was why she'd been spying on Oliver from Grand Central; unfortunately, from what she'd seen so far, he was chummy with Miles McLaughlin and Kevin Hall. Maybe that didn't mean anything, though. The men were co-workers, after all.

Still, all this had thrown a wrench into her plans to contact Oliver, and now she felt even more ambivalent about going to the police. Why was an FBI agent chasing her? Her eyes darting, she searched the street as people surged around her. Oliver couldn't have gone far. Moments ago, she'd tried to get closer to him by crossing the street, but both sides of Sixth Avenue were barricaded by police officers and sawhorses. Oliver had to be as trapped by the crowds as she.

The parade was a sight to behold, nothing like the well-known Macy's parade. Here, in Greenwich Village, the atmosphere was more akin to Mardi Gras. Downtown revelers were costumed, dressed as turkeys, pilgrims and Native Americans. Irreverently ignoring the usual solemnity of the family holiday, the merrymakers scattered firecrackers in the street while a jazz band played the *Wizard of Oz* theme song.

She glanced around nervously. Oliver had seemed to recognize her in the subway, but maybe he'd just been running late and trying to catch a train. Now, even though she was wearing a simple, black Lone Ranger's mask she'd bought from a street vendor, she feared the disguise would never fool Oliver Vargo, much less Susan Jones. Was the woman looking for her? If Peggy was found, would Susan try taking another shot?

Stress was taking its toll. Shivering, Peggy wished she'd eaten dinner. She was hungry and cold, even though the temperature was hovering in the forties. The wind had picked up, turning brisk, and the rain had tapered to an icy drizzle. The skimpy white dress beneath her coat had gotten damp.

She hugged her arms around herself. "Where are you?" she whispered again. How, in all this madness, was she supposed to find Oliver? She could only pray he wasn't really as friendly with Miles as he'd looked when she'd spied on them. If it was Peggy's word against Miles's, who would Oliver be most inclined to believe? Peggy Fox, whom he'd never even met— or one of his own colleagues, a man he lunched with every day?

Shoving ungloved hands deep into the raincoat's pockets, Peggy shivered again. Despite the body heat enveloping her, the gutters were gushing and her feet were soaked. She wanted to return to the hotel, take a shower and dry her wet clothes on the steam-heat registers. Just as she turned, preparing to fight her way through the crowd and back to the hotel, a hand curled around her upper arm.

Susan Jones! Fear bubbled in her throat as the fingers tightened purposefully. The woman had found her! Peggy was about to die! Her body tensed, and her throat closed in panic. She waited to feel a gun prodding her ribs. Cocking her head, she strained her ears. She didn't know what command she expected. *Don't say a word, Ms. Fox. Just do exactly as I say,* maybe. Or, *One wrong move and you're history.* Or even worse, *If you tell anyone what you know, your mom and Aunt Jill will pay.*

She wished with all her heart that she hadn't caught Miles in bed with Susan Jones—and that she hadn't seen the money in the suitcase. Pain sliced through her. Her mom and Aunt Jill would be devastated if something bad happened to her. She'd do anything she could to protect them. When no one spoke, she tried unsuccessfully to wrench around, realizing in the process that the tall, hard body pressed against her back was decidedly male, which meant it wasn't Susan Jones.

Was it Miles? Had she spoken his name aloud? She was so scared, Peggy wasn't sure. Or was this his sidekick, the black man, Kevin Hall? Trapped by the crowd, she couldn't turn. Or run. Or hide.

She squirmed, but every inch of the man's muscular body moved with her. It was definitely the wrong time to notice how well suited she and this stranger were, at least from a physical perspective. His thighs molded to hers, his lap curved over her behind, his solar plexus fit into the groove of her spine, and finally, the steady thud of his heart seemed to take up residence inside her own chest, in the space just below her left shoulder.

Her pulse was racing, and when she sucked in another breath, hoping to calm herself, she knew it was useless. The man leaned closer, angled his head down, and she felt his breath against her neck; in the cold night, it was as warm as a fire. Suddenly, her heart ached. A wave of homesickness brought tears to her eyes. Blinking, she whispered, "Stop."

He didn't move or say a word. His breath kept teasing her, though—stirring strands of hair that traced her neck and the curve of her ear. What was going on? Was some crazy stranger about to try to steal a kiss? Was some psycho behind her? Half expecting his tongue to trace the shell of her ear, she felt her pulse catapult, jolting over the top.

"Gotcha," he whispered simply.

Oliver Vargo.

She'd never felt the man's touch before, but she'd recognize his voice anywhere. The distinctive bass was exactly as it had sounded during his televised interviews—and it sent a shiver of longing down her spine. He must have caught her watching him and doubled back to confront her.

"What are you doing?" she managed to say, ignoring traitorous sensations as she craned her neck to look over her shoulder.

"What are *you* doing?" he returned, his low voice dropping a seductive notch as his fingers flexed around her arm. "That might be a better place to start."

Jerking her head in his direction, she struggled to

keep her voice noncommittal. "I'm watching the parade."

"Following me," he countered.

Silently, she berated herself. Of course he'd noticed. He was an FBI agent—and one of the best. Oh, that day in the subway, she'd worried that he'd seen her, but she'd told herself that throwing her hair in front of her face had worked as a disguise. *Guess not.*

Oblivious of how his physical proximity was affecting her, he inched closer, and her heart missed a beat as heat flooded her. Yes, this was definitely the wrong time to contemplate how many fantasies she'd had about him rescuing her....

But she'd had plenty. Which was why, when the crowd behind him swelled, pushing him against her, she knew the man wasn't really aroused. Oh, no. She was the one who'd been fantasizing about him—not the other way around. What Peggy felt was the result of her overactive imagination. Nevertheless, hadn't she felt...*something?* And before she could stop herself, hadn't that hard, powerful *something* brought a soft sigh to her lips? Well, no matter how sexy Oliver was, she had to stay in control. She had to keep her wits about her, in case whatever had prompted Kevin Hall to chase her might also prompt Oliver to...

On a surge of fear, she pivoted. Struggling as a second arm circled her, she continued fighting. She was sorry she did, too, because all the maneuvering brought the front of her body flush with his—and while Oliver wasn't exactly aroused, he wasn't not-aroused, either. Even more unsettling, she found herself gazing into his heart-stopping eyes. Darker than on television, they looked the color of liquid ink in the night, and they were scrutinizing her without apology.

"Let me go," she said, trying to tell herself that the male awareness she saw was only her own wishful thinking.

When he didn't release her, she swallowed hard. Was he helping Miles McLaughlin and Kevin Hall find her? Moving on instinct, she tried to run again, but there was nowhere to go. Oliver reflexively drew her nearer, and her cheek wound up pressed against a white shirt he wore beneath his trench coat. Heady scents assaulted her. He smelled just the way a man should.

Veering back, she slammed a fist to his chest, using the wall of muscle to steady herself, vaguely aware that her own coat was opening in the process. When she registered his skin quivering under her fingertips, she snatched back her hand. Inhaling audibly, she said, "Could you give me some breathing room?"

"Don't worry," he retorted dryly, his gaze flicking over the low-cut white dress she'd exposed. "I won't burn you."

"I doubt that," she grumbled. Fighting embarrassment, she drew together the sides of the coat, knowing the lace of her bra had been visible through the dress's tight fabric. No doubt, he'd noticed the effects of the chill air, too. She considered telling him that the dress didn't even belong to her, but that would only call attention to the outfit and make matters worse.

"You doubt that? What do you mean?"

She shook her head. "Nothing."

But no TV image could have prepared her for how Oliver Vargo would affect her in real life. She'd already noted that his eyes seemed darker, as liquid as the November night, and yet they were full of glinting fire. Feeling completely unsettled, she tried to ignore how those eyes were roving over her face, as if memorizing each contour. "Why don't you take off the mask?"

"Why?"

"I want to see your eyes."

At the thought of Oliver Vargo scrutinizing her further, a shiver went down her spine, and she was glad for the mask. "I'd take it off, but everybody here's in costume if you didn't notice."

"I noticed."

"Then where's your mask?"

"Must have left it at home."

It would be a pity to cover those eyes. No, interviews hadn't prepared Peggy for how the drizzle would look in his hair; glistening droplets caught in the thick, black waves, refracting light. How he towered over her was a surprise, too, since she was nearly six feet tall, herself, and men never did. The power coiling in his body wasn't anticipated, either. Heat seeped from beneath his clothes, and as it warmed her, she wanted nothing more than to cup her hands over his broad shoulders and let him carry her away....

She came to her senses. "C'mon," she repeated. "Let me go."

His hand curled more tightly around her arm. "Go where?"

She said the first thing that came to mind. It was what she most wanted, after all. To be back in Ohio, watching her mother knit while Aunt Jill made one of the apple pies she was so well known for. "Home."

"And where exactly is that?"

She should have known he wasn't the kind of guy who liked one-word answers. Still startled by his sudden appearance, she said the next thing that popped into her head. "How did you get over here, anyway? You were across the street."

"So, you're definitely following me."

"I thought you knew that."

"I'm still waiting to hear why."

"I'm not really following you," she protested. "I mean, I…uh…"

His hand flexed in warning, and her mind hazed. Something black seemed to seep in at the edges of her consciousness. What *was* she about to say? With Oliver so close, she really couldn't remember. She tried to focus, but only found herself concentrating on the warm hand curled around the sleeve of her coat. His fingers were long, slender and tapered. That was something else she hadn't anticipated. Oliver Vargo had the hands of an artist.

"How did you get over here?" She managed to begin speaking again even though her throat was tight. "Sixth Avenue was blocked off on both sides." The instant she said it, she realized he'd probably flashed his badge, but he surprised her again.

"I bought a token and went underground."

He'd crossed beneath the street, using the subway concourse. "Smart move."

"I'm full of them."

"And modest."

"So they say."

"What's your name?" she retorted. Maybe that would throw him off the track. Maybe it was best if she pretended not to know anything about him.

"I think you already know," he said calmly. "But it's Oliver. Oliver Vargo."

The way he said it reminded her of how James Bond always introduced himself. *The name's Bond, James Bond.* His fleeting smile didn't quite reach his eyes, although it did show off rows of straight, white, gleaming teeth. Days ago, she'd decided he was more interesting-looking than handsome, but now that he was inches away, she was changing her mind. He was mouthwatering. Too bad he wasn't acting nearly as charming as when he was on television, chatting with Kate Olsen.

"And since we're exchanging names…" he said.

Despite his annoyance, his voice rippled through her, sending heat into her bloodstream, shooting quill after quivering quill into her belly.

"You were outside Grand Central," he continued. "And outside the apartment where I'm staying, watching me from a club across the street, Nite-Lite."

Yes, indeed, Oliver was more observant than she'd realized. He had a very commanding presence, too, and she was beginning to understand that denying all the accusations might not be in her best interest. Still, days ago, she'd been ready to turn to him for help, but now, after spying on him from Grand Central, she needed to be more certain she could trust him. "I can explain everything," she said cautiously.

"I'm waiting." When she didn't respond immediately, he added dryly, "No rush. We've got all night."

"We won't have to spend all night," she said quickly.

"We won't be spending the night," he murmured in soft echo, seemingly liking how the innuendo made her eyes widen.

"That's not what I meant."

"What did you mean?"

Now that she was getting over her shock, Peggy noticed Oliver was looking at her with an oddly curious expression, as if he'd seen her somewhere before. "I don't know where to start," she said.

"You said you could explain everything," he retorted, his gaze still assessing. "So, why don't you start with that?" he suggested. "Everything."

Surely she was misinterpreting the strange look in his eyes, but he clearly recognized her. There was no mistaking it now. Had Miles McLaughlin told him about her? And why had Kevin Hall chased her? she wondered again, panic making her insides tighten. "Before I do," she said, "I need to know why you're looking at me like that."

"Like what?"

Like you know me. And like you want to kiss me. The thought came unbidden, but she could see it in the way his eyes kept drifting to her mouth. In fact, his eyes seemed to devour her, as if he'd long had fantasies about her. That was crazy, of course, and she tried to tell herself it was only wishful thinking, since she'd dreamed of him. What woman wouldn't? Peggy was healthy. And sexually active before she'd sworn off love.

"Have we met before?" he asked.

"Have we?" she managed.

"I've seen you," he murmured. "The same dark eyes. The same blond hair…"

Something in his voice—a thread of steel weaving through softness—made her heart pound again. As it beat a tattoo against her ribs, she wished with all her strength that he'd let her go. If anything convinced her she'd made a huge mistake by following him, it was the weakness hitting the backs of her knees. Yes, with his hard, aroused body pressed against hers, she suddenly felt sorry, truly sorry, they'd met. As things stood, she'd been in enough trouble.

"Let me go," she said again, with more conviction.

"I don't think so," he answered in an easy tone that belied his commanding words. "You're coming with me, Cameron."

Things were getting stranger by the minute. She swallowed nervously. "Cameron?"

"Yeah…" Lightly licking his lips, he repeated the name as if he liked the taste of it in his mouth. "Cameron."

"What are you talking a—"

He interrupted, saying the strangest thing yet. "Whoever you are—" He squeezed his hand around her arm again as if to test the truth of it. "You're every bit as real as me."

"Of course I am." She squinted at him.

"Why are you following me?" he asked again.

"Look," she said, "I don't mean you any harm—"

"You," he emphasized with a chuckle. "Harm *me?"*

Of course the idea was ludicrous. Oliver Vargo was tall, broad-shouldered and packed with solid muscle that made her shudder. "I didn't mean to imply you couldn't defend yourself." The question was, could he defend *her?*

The longer she looked at him, she wasn't even sure she wanted him to. The second their bodies connected, she'd realized this man could be dangerous, if only to her heart. How many times could a woman trust, after all? How many times could she heal and then open herself up to let in feelings of love—only to find out she'd been used again?

She bit down hard on her lower lip. Everything around her seemed to tilt off-kilter. Admit it, she thought. She was already half in love with him. She was a crime-story junkie, which was what had gotten her into all this trouble in the first place, and when she'd read Oliver's books she'd been smitten…

Her eyes darted from left to right, seeking escape.

"Don't even think about it," he warned quietly.

She wanted to look anywhere but into his eyes, and yet she forced herself to stare him down, not about to be intimidated. "Why did you call me Cameron?"

"What *is* your name?"

"I see you're going to answer questions with questions."

"Until you start talking."

She considered a long moment. Feeling sure nothing good was going to come of all this, she said, "I guess Cameron will do. For now." Maybe this way, she could buy time, find out what was happening at the FBI office. Whatever was going through Oliver Vargo's mind at the moment, he wasn't saying he was going to take her in for questioning, the way Kevin Hall had....

"Who are you, really?"

She had a thousand answers for that, beginning with Peggy Fox, a woman in trouble. But he was getting impatient. He said, "Are you a fan?"

"Uh...yeah." *That, too.*

His gaze flicked down, making her realize her coat had fallen open again. He was slowly perusing the tight white dress beneath, his gaze lingering on the scoop neckline, as if he was thoroughly intrigued by the space where fabric ended and skin began.

The crowd surged, pushing him into her arms, and she gasped. Her hands dropped the coat collar and grabbed the sawhorse behind her. Trapped against the barricade, she felt completely helpless when their hips locked. When his chest brushed hers, there was no help for the way her nipples beaded. Heat flooded her cheeks, staining them a crimson red that even the night's darkness couldn't hide. He seemed to be aware of every nuance. She was sure of it when she registered his quickening breath.

"Look," she managed to say. "We can't talk here." In this cold rain, her white dress might as well be made of cellophane.

His intrigued expression didn't bring much comfort. "You have a better idea?"

The seconds seemed to drag on—as if this whole

exchange had lasted an eternity, not a scant few minutes. Apparently, Oliver Vargo thought she was a crazed fan.

Dammit, she *was* a fan.

But not the one he assumed. Had he had some difficulty with a woman named Cameron? Whatever the case, he didn't know her *real* name, which meant Miles McLaughlin hadn't mentioned her to him. Regarding his and Miles's relationship, there was only one way to find out the truth—question him. "I...I have a hotel."

He stared at her. "Did you say hotel?"

She nodded toward McDougal Street. "I'm in the Washington Square Hotel." It was only two blocks away. She'd been so intent on gauging the distance that she'd barely noticed the genuine smile claiming Oliver's lips. When she saw it, she felt thoroughly unsettled. All at once, the man's countenance had cleared. He offered a slight nod, as if a knotty misunderstanding had been resolved and everything now made perfect sense to him.

Good for you, Peggy thought dryly, since *she* still didn't have a clue what was going on.

His hand slid slowly downward, gliding from her upper arm to her elbow, creating a wake of electrical current. A brass band began to play, and over the music, Oliver softly repeated the word *hotel*. And then, under his breath, he added, "Cameron, this is a dream come true."

4

CAMERON WAS SEDUCING him, Oliver thought moments later, loosening his grasp on her elbow as they went through a brass revolving door that spit them into a hotel lobby. At first, he'd thought the woman might be a fan, but that didn't explain how her picture had wound up on his PC screen. Which meant she must be a friend of his sister's. Anna had been doing everything she could to fix him up with one of her friends, and this was obviously part of a scheme cooked up by the two women. Anna must have fed the picture of her friend into his computer, convincing him that the woman was America's Sexiest Woman, all so that he'd be excited when the woman actually appeared.

"Home sweet home," she said.

The idea that she was trying to get him into bed had calmed Oliver considerably. He glanced around. Long past its glory days, the red-carpeted lobby was decorated with marble-top tables and chandeliers. Outside, the streets surrounding the parade had sounded like Bourbon Street in New Orleans on a Saturday night, so only when Oliver squeezed into a rickety, dimly lit elevator with Cameron did he fully register the comparative deafening silence. "Quiet in here," he offered.

As she pushed the seventh-floor button, he noted her nails were painted opal, not love-me red as they had been in both her picture and his fantasies. He tried not to feel too disappointed, but it was difficult when she'd appeared so often in his dreams, raking those fingertips over his body. At nothing more than the thought, his breath turned shallow with anticipation.

"Dark, too," she supplied.

He heard the faintest quiver in her voice, and the answering flutter of his heart took him by surprise. Whoever this woman was, she probably didn't make a habit of seducing men, judging by her nervousness. And yet she'd chosen him.

He sent her an encouraging smile. "The elevator could use a new lightbulb," he conceded.

She didn't answer.

But he wasn't put off by her lack of response. In fact, he was feeling uncharacteristically anxious himself. Who wouldn't? He was about to have sex with a stranger, after all. Why else would the woman ask him to her hotel room? And she wasn't quite a stranger, he mentally corrected. She was a friend of Anna's.

Suppressing a shudder, he remembered how she'd felt pressed against him in the street—how the curves of her backside had risen, cushioning his groin, and how the harder ridges of her hips had collided with his when she'd whirled around. Their lower bodies had clicked, and now the memory sent heat prancing across his skin.

Yeah, while they'd been on Sixth Avenue, he'd realized she had to be a friend of his sister's—there was simply no other reasonable explanation—and now, with her standing so close, and her scent driving him wild in the cramped elevator, he wished he'd been nicer. Could he help it if he'd been worried, though? She'd been tailing him...

Oliver broadened his smile as he tucked down the collar of his coat, allowing the rainwater to roll off. "And wet," he added. Another uncomfortable moment passed before the smile twitched his lips and he continued. "The elevator's slow, too."

His comical efforts to make conversation solicited a low, barely audible laugh from her. "At this rate," she murmured, lifting a hand to reposition the eye mask, a fashion accessory that had been heightening his excitement immeasurably, "we won't reach the seventh floor until tomorrow."

"Midnight," he countered. His eyes said he could think of countless things he and his masked date might do to amuse themselves during the wait.

"Midnight," she echoed.

He flicked his gaze down her body. "I'm an optimist," he assured.

"Really?"

"Really."

Yeah, this strange little encounter was definitely going to end with them in bed together, he thought, his pulse quickening. If he was lucky, maybe the affair would even develop into something more. With an unexpected twinge of emotion, he thought of the house he'd built near his office in Quantico, then he pushed away the image. He'd be satisfied if this love game just lasted through Christmas so he wouldn't wind up spending the holiday alone.

She'd fixed her gaze studiously on the elevator buttons, but the black mask couldn't hide how her eyes drifted again to choice parts of his anatomy. He shook his head in bemusement, recalling how Anna had come to his office, slyly bribing him with lunch while running the Sex Files through his Quick Composite software, just so she could pull up a picture of her friend, this woman. No doubt, Vic, who was a whiz with cameras and optical illusions, had helped her with this.

Along with producing "Cameron's" picture, Anna had stuffed condoms into his wallet, too. Cameron— maybe that was even her real name—was showing herself to be every bit as adventurous. Even as he admired the woman's face, he was giving her points for ingenuity. She'd almost made him—a completely rational law enforcement agent—believe that an image of America's sexiest woman had come to life.

It wasn't every day that such a gorgeous, intelligent woman went to so much trouble for his benefit. Sexually, she must want him badly. Not only had she followed him all over Manhattan, wearing slinky clothes, but she'd rented a hotel room. Silently, he cursed the elevator for going so slow. He couldn't wait to see her lying on her back in bed. Her gaze locked with his, and before she glanced away, he saw desire flare in her eyes, naked and bright.

He parted his lips to speak. Then they both started

talking at once with him saying, "Look, I'm sorry I scared you—"

"Out there," she quickly clarified. "You just caught me off guard. Like I said, I can explain—"

"I didn't mean to, but—"

"None of this is what it seems—"

Just as he thought she'd tell him she was Anna's friend, she stopped talking. Uncertain, her smile remained fixed on her lips. It wasn't exactly a come-hither expression, but his mouth turned cottony, anyway. His palms itched. Her picture didn't do her justice.

Wind and drizzle had tightened the loose waves of her hair, curling the ends like ribbons. The strands looked even darker than they had outside, the color of things that didn't belong in New York City—wheat in a farm field at night, syrupy honey drenching a warm honeycomb, wet straw scattered on the floor of a hayloft. Much of her face was covered by the mask, but the skin Oliver could see was alight with a healthy, ruddy glow. He didn't bother to hide his appreciative gaze. Why should he? She was seducing him, right?

Even the closed raincoat couldn't conceal her full figure. She'd belted the coat tightly as they'd run for the hotel, accentuating the nip of her waist. The hem hit shapely calves, and smooth legs shimmered through sheer stockings she wore with black pumps. Oliver could almost see himself, just moments from now, wiggling each shoe from a slender foot before tugging those stockings down legs he knew would be as smooth as satin. Heat swirling in his lower belly, he pictured her upper thighs, imagining how black garters would look on her water-smooth skin. Was she wearing panties? What color?

Once more, his dreams came flooding back, and unbidden, he was remembering the blush of her breasts, lathered in mentholated oil. The elevator seemed to explode with the scent of mint, and his body tensed. He was about to act on impulse, step closer and haul her into his arms, when she suddenly said, "You had every right to confront me."

The elevator had paused, its doors laboriously opening onto a vacant hallway, then shutting again. Pulleys groaned as the car heaved, lurching upward once more. "Believe me," she continued, "I know how unnerving it can be when someone's following you—"

Now that he was sure she was Anna's friend, he'd rather progress the relationship, not dwell on apologies. Hearing her teeth chatter, he murmured, "Don't worry about it. You must be freezing. Let's get upstairs and get you warm."

"You don't have to be so nice about this," she said guiltily. "I *have* been following you."

"Yeah." He sent her another smile. "And I caught you."

"As I said, I can explain—"

"No need. I understand now. The question is, what are we going to do next?"

Before she could respond, the doors opened. Gliding a hand beneath her elbow, he steered her into the hallway. "Which room?"

Her voice sounded shaky. "Uh…712."

When they reached the door, she inserted a key card, then pushed open the door and entered. She was halfway across the room when she turned to face him. "Here we are."

Drawing a deep breath to steady himself, Oliver felt he could barely move. Only the bathroom light was on. Deeper in the room, where she now stood, everything looked as dark and soft as chocolate. She looked as tasty, too.

Beautiful. That was another word for her. Quick Composite had only given him a picture with which to fantasize, but now they were off the busy streets and out of the rain, and he could take a better look at her. Or at least he could once they turned on the light.

"Sit down if you'd like," she said.

The words skated along his nerves, rippling all the way to their endings. "Thanks," he murmured without moving.

The room, like so many in Manhattan where space was at a premium, was tiny. A mirrored closet door was open, and he could see a chest of drawers, as well as a duffel. A TV was recessed into the wall; other than a bedside table, there was no furniture, only a queen-size bed. Behind her was a tiny bathroom, and the only window was covered with a heavy curtain. City lights didn't penetrate, but he could hear muffled sounds of traffic.

Shutting the door behind him, he flashed a grin in the near darkness. "Lived here long?"

"Just since this evening."

She'd backed so far into the room that between her dark coat and mask, she seemed to fade into the darkness. Glancing at the bed, he wondered if she'd want to talk first, or get right down to business. He said, "I see."

Her voice sounded strangely small. "I'm not sure you do, Mr. Vargo."

"Under the circumstances, you can call me Oliver."

Squinting, he watched as she slowly unbelted her coat, giving him a glimpse of the rain-damp, nearly transparent white dress she wore beneath. "Look," she began, "we need to talk. I mean, uh, I'm a little confused. What exactly do you think the circumstances *are?*"

"I figure the circumstances are whatever we make them," he said cautiously. "What say, we order room service and talk it over?"

She considered. "Sure. Uh…feel free to hang your coat in the closet."

In his line of work, he'd learned to identify accents, but hers was hard to place. He heard rolling cadences, as if she'd spent time abroad and spoke several languages, but there was also something sharper, suggesting she'd been in New York for a long time. Beneath that, he'd noticed flat vowels. "Where are you from? Ohio?"

She'd been clutching the open ends of her belt, and now she toyed with them nervously. "What makes you say that?"

"Your accent."

"Oh."

Her obvious relief took him aback. Didn't she intend to let him get to know her? Or was this unusual night just meant to be a fantasy come true? The idea bothered him more than he wanted to admit. He didn't even know the woman, but he was interested. He hadn't so much as kissed her, yet he wanted to know what kind of woman would want to play America's Sexiest Woman with a near stranger.

"I think we need some background noise," she suddenly murmured, picking up the remote control and flicking on a channel.

"The Home Shopping Network doesn't really set the right tone," he countered. When she merely stared, as if she was afraid to ask what *would,* he added, "What about music?"

"Music?" Her voice wavered as if she'd never heard of such a thing.

His lips quirked. "It's that thing with notes. Bars. Scales."

"Right," she said breathily. "I've heard of that."

His heart squeezed. At the parade she'd seemed scrappy and full of chutzpah, but now that they were alone in a hotel room, she apparently wasn't quite sure what to do. That touched him even more than all the effort she, Anna and Vic must have put into this charade. Edging toward a clock radio on the bedside table, he said, "Here. I'll find us something. Any preferences?"

"You pick."

Something soft, romantic and made for slow, sweet seduction, he decided. As he fiddled with the radio dial, he shrugged out of his coat, feeling her eyes on his back. "Here. Hand me the remote."

He took it without looking at her, and as he did, their fingers brushed. A tingling sensation spread from the point of contact all the way up his arm. If there was any proof they belonged skin to skin it was this. No other woman's touch had ever gotten him so hot with anticipation. A moment later he found a station that suited him, and as jazz filled the room, he flicked on the lamp.

And then he turned around. He was prepared for the vision of his dream lover, who was wearing nothing but that shimmering, see-through dress and, he hoped, no panties...

But stronger light transformed the dream vision.

His jaw slackened, and he could only stare in shock. Her practical green raincoat was streaked and limp. Hair that had appeared love-tousled in the night's smoky darkness now looked bedraggled. Silk stockings that had seemed deliciously sheer, were mud-splashed, and black dye from her pumps had bled onto the hose, creating a dark, uneven water line around her ankles. He thought he could see hints of smeared mascara under her eyes.

She shivered.

"You're soaked," he murmured.

"It's raining," she defended. "Or didn't you notice?"

"My mind was on other things," he admitted. Namely her.

Despite his concern, he felt a pang at his groin when he realized it was his job to help her out of all those wet clothes. What was he doing standing here like an idiot? Crossing the room, he draped his own coat over his arm. "Here," he murmured again, settling his hands on her shoulders and gently urging her to take off her wrap. "You need to get out of this."

Her hands flew to the lapels, and her eyes widened behind the mask. He didn't blame her for the modesty. Outside, the game of seduction was one thing. Inside, he was about to see her in a dress so damp and tight that nothing would be left to the imagination.

"I'm fine," she said softly.

"You're freezing," he countered.

"It was cold outside."

His voice turned husky. "I know. But we're inside now. C'mon. Take off the coat."

Conceding with an audible sigh, she let him push the sleeves down her arms. As he did, his breath caught. She was drenched, all right. White fabric clung to breasts made even fuller by the underwire of a bra. Cold, her nipples had grown tight—painfully tight—he imagined, and in need of the hot ministrations of his mouth. He yearned to touch and devour. Everything about the night kicked up another dizzying notch when he saw the outline of thin black straps circling her hips. So much for the idea that she wasn't wearing panties. A triangular sliver of fabric was so visible that it had rendered the dress superfluous.

"Really," she managed to say as he ignored the grasp she had on her coat and eased it away from her. "I don't need help."

"You can say that again," he murmured appreciatively. He'd never seen anybody look sexier. She was still wearing the eye mask, and the brown eyes staring at him from behind it looked astonishingly innocent.

Just as he turned with both coats, heading for the closet, he could swear he heard her stomach growl. Frowning, he asked over his shoulder, "Did you eat dinner?"

"Not much," she admitted.

"What did you have?"

There was a long pause. "Crackers."

His frown deepening, he felt anger flare briefly. Once more, he should have known. She was just like Anna. Too full of adventure to take proper care of herself. No matter how intent she'd been on playing out this delicious sexual fantasy—something he wasn't exactly going to complain about—she should have eaten. "Crackers?"

"And peanut butter."

"Nutritious," he returned dryly.

"What?" she muttered, dragging a hand through her damp hair. She patted the sides as if suddenly realizing the strands were in wild disarray. "Are you a dietician?"

"Hardly. You know what I do for a living." From the closet door, he shot a glance over his shoulder. "What do you do, anyway?"

"Lots of things. Why?"

"Because the way things stand, you've got all the advantages."

"Such as?"

"Anna's probably told you everything about me."

"Who's Anna?"

Ah. So she was going to play it that way. "Fine," he said. "Have it your way. We'll just pretend you materialized off a computer screen."

At her stupefied expression, he found himself biting back a chuckle. The woman was definitely good at toying with him. He had to give her that.

"I'm not sure we're on the same wavelength," she said.

He would have responded, but when he turned to hang up their coats, his gaze landed on the open duffel on the closet's floor. Sucking in a quick breath, he took in the panorama of sexy lingerie inside. "You'd better get undressed before you catch pneumonia," he managed to say, imagining her wearing the garter belt or sheer body suit. Suddenly, he knew he couldn't stand much more of this. He wanted this wild woman in bed. Now. Leaning, he fished in the duffel and lifted out a pair of black Lycra pants and a net shirt with an inbuilt bra.

"Undressed?" she asked as he turned around.

He smiled as he moved toward her, deciding it was long past time to test the waters and see if this encounter was really heading where he suspected. "With or without me."

Her voice hitched. "Excuse me?"

He parted his lips to speak, but heard her shiver again, and so, when he reached her, he simply hooked a finger under the elastic band of the black eye mask and lifted it over her head. For a second, he could scarcely breathe. Seeing her face affected him even more than seeing every blessed detail of her body. She had the face of an angel—with high cheekbones, round cheeks and inviting lips that had been reddened by the cold. "Yeah," he said, rubbing her arms to warm her before handing her the clothes. "You're freezing."

"It's chilly out," she said again.

He nodded toward the bathroom, but she barely seemed to notice. She was staring down at the outfit he'd chosen, which was small enough to fit into the palm of her hand. A flush rose on her cheeks. "I can't wear these."

He started to point out that her current attire was even more revealing. "They're your clothes."

"I know, but…"

"Would you prefer something else?"

She swallowed hard. "I don't have anything else."

Judging from her mournful expression, he'd bet she was wishing for jeans and a sweatshirt. And while the wet dress and Lycra pants were striking his every male chord, he suddenly wondered how she'd look in ordinary clothes. Cute, he decided. Sexy as hell. And yet he was deeply moved that this woman would go this far to seduce him. "Really," he said when her teeth chattered. "You need to change. If you don't, you're going to wind up getting sick. This time of year, there are a lot of viruses around."

She was still blushing, probably because she knew she might as well be standing in front of him naked. A frustrated sigh came from between her lips. "Will you be okay while I…"

"Don't worry about me. I'll order some food. Consider it dessert for those crackers you had for dinner."

She looked relieved. "Food. That would be great, Oliver."

It was the first time she'd used his name, and he liked the familiar way she said it, as if he'd been in her thoughts for a good long while. She'd certainly been in his ever since Anna had fed her picture into his computer. "Take your time."

"I won't be long."

His eyes drifted to where the shoe dye had ruined her hose. "Take a shower if you want."

Another wave of relief was visible. "Really? Are you sure you don't…"

"Mind?" Shaking his head, he smiled. "Not at all. This is one of the strangest encounters of my life."

"Mine, too."

"So, let's make the most of it. Just go with the flow. By the time you're out of the shower, dinner will be served."

As she retreated to the bathroom, he bit back a low whistle of appreciation. She had a great back. Hell, the woman had a great everything. When he didn't hear a lock sliding into place, he tilted his head and considered. Was he supposed to follow her? Was this part of her seduction plan?

Unsure, he picked up a room-service menu, but couldn't decide what to order. Heading for the bathroom, he leaned toward the door, bringing his lips near the crack. As he listened to the running shower, he blew out another breath. He could almost see Cameron, right on the other side of the door, naked and waiting for him.

"Cameron?"

Her voice was unusually bright. "Be right there!"

"No rush," he assured. "But what do you want to eat?"

"I...I don't know." She sounded nervous. "I'll have whatever you're having."

Staring down at the menu again, he realized he was starving, too. He'd worked late, then gone directly to the parade. "What about some aphrodisiacs?"

"I can't hear you," she called. "Just get whatever you want."

He knew exactly what he wanted—her. But first, he lifted the phone, dialed room service and ordered the night's special—a Thanksgiving dinner with all the trimmings. In case that didn't suffice, he added oysters, artichoke hearts, desserts richly laced with chocolate syrup and two bottles of champagne. "That ought to cover it," he whispered.

"How long?" he asked the room-service attendant.

"Sorry, sir. We're rushed. Probably an hour."

"That decides things then," said Oliver.

And then he kicked off his shoes, unbuttoned his shirt and shrugged out of it, stepped out of his slacks and briefs, and headed for the bathroom.

5

As THE SHOWER CURTAIN opened, Peggy instinctively stepped backward, covering her breasts. Just as instinctively, her gaze lowered. Her heart hammered at the sight of Oliver Vargo. Naked and aroused, he was stepping over the lip of the tub.

"What are you doing?" she sputtered through the stream of water coursing from the nozzle of a shower massage dangling above her head.

His dark eyes sparked with devilment. "What do you think, Cameron?"

The truth was, she couldn't. And this was definitely the wrong moment to explain that her name wasn't Cameron. She was too busy staring at him. His skin was darker than she'd imagined. Smooth, too, except for where black hair bisected hard pectorals. His chest was ribbed, his belly flat, his hips narrow. Unable to help herself, she followed the dark tangled curls to where they ended in a riotous mass. Everything inside her tightened when she took in the rest. She quickly raised her eyes to his—and wished she hadn't.

Oliver Vargo was grinning, staring back at her with interest, his eyes searching her face. "I didn't figure you'd mind if I joined you," he said simply, his voice low and sexy.

Under other circumstances, the man's confidence might have been annoying, but Peggy had been on the run. For too long now, she'd felt tired and scared. Just seconds before, she'd had her eyes shut, her head tilted backward; water had been pelting her face, its heat thawing her chilled body—and all because Oliver Vargo was standing guard outside the door like an avenging angel. Now she was vaguely aware that her hair was lathered, her body coated with suds, and that a bar of soap was about to slip from her hand. "Uh…"

"Here." He reached out a hairy forearm. "Why don't you let me take that?"

Long tapered fingers stroked the back of her hand, and then he turned over her palm. As she let the soap slip through her fingers into his, unexpected emotion claimed her. It came from nowhere, and she was glad he couldn't see the tears springing to her eyes under the deluge of water. Yes, just knowing he was outside the bathroom door, she'd felt safe for the first time in days. She could shower in peace, change into warm, dry clothes, and with him nearby, eat a complete meal.

He unsettled her, but he comforted her, too. And now Oliver Vargo—a man she didn't even know…a man who'd been the object of her fantasies—had joined her in the shower.

Gently, he eased her hands from her chest, and even as she reminded herself that she'd meant to talk to him about Miles and Susan Jones, she lowered her hands to her sides, letting Oliver look his fill. Her mind raced. She really needed to tell him why she'd been following him before it was too late.

"You're beautiful," he murmured. Eyes as hot as flames and as dark as coals drifted ravenously over her skin, soliciting a shiver from her. Before setting the soap bar aside, he sudsed his hands then splayed them on her rib cage.

At the contact, her breath caught. "This is crazy. We don't even know—"

His mouth stopped her. Under rushing water, his lips settled on hers, locking perfectly, just the way his body promised to. Firm and sure, it moved slowly, parting her lips, then nibbling. She could scarcely believe any of this was happening. Had Oliver Vargo really just stepped into a hot shower with her? *Unreal.*

A moan rose in her throat as his lathered hands drifted upward, catching beneath her breasts as he deepened the kiss. Lifting them, he tested their weight, then his hands turned slippery again and rushed over her breasts like the rivulets from the shower nozzle. In tandem with the slow, sensual thrusts of his tongue, he stroked the sides, then covered the mounds in white bubbles. As he pushed them together, he uttered a soft groan of male satisfaction.

Her already hard nipples further tightened while the surging push of his tongue inside her mouth sent liquid heat shooting to her core. The thrust of his hips followed. Hot and throbbing, his erection sought her, pushing between thighs she parted for him. He surged there, too—another promise—and she released an answering gasp of need.

"Please," she whispered hoarsely.

"Not yet."

Using only his nail, he found a breast again and flicked a taut peak, his mouth quickly capturing the very cry he coaxed from her. Her knees weakened. He'd caught her so off guard! And she needed this so badly: she needed his strong arms, and this impulsive lovemaking to make her forget the nightmare she'd been living.

Her lips parted farther—now in protest—when he broke the kiss. But he ignored her. Lowering his head, he leaned and flicked his tongue against the nipple. Again and again, the tip strobed against her flesh until every inch of her yearned.

Her pulse raced. No man had ever aroused her so quickly, or so deeply. But there was no time to wonder at the intensity. It was taking her by storm. Sweeping over her and buffeting her insides, the sensations were making her shaky, wild. Images of sexual things she'd like to do with him rushed through her mind—she saw herself stroking his penis until he was begging for release...saw herself going down on her knees to draw him deeply between her lips.

Gasping, she circled her arms tightly around his waist; clinging to him, she threw her head back, surrendering. He cupped a large hand around the back of her neck then, and his fingers climbed upward, grasping strands of soaked hair. He tugged almost roughly, using the leverage to pull her mouth down hard onto his once more. He was hungry. Each onslaught of his mouth, each fresh thrust of his tongue drew her in deeper until she was drowning in a world of spiraling temptation.

His breath was shallow, coming in a soft, panting rasp as he curled fingers over her breast and squeezed. Beyond the sound of water beating past her ears and onto her shoulders, she could hear the soft sounds of jazz, and for a second, it sent her catapulting back to her senses. But then she gasped again, powerless to fight the slippery fingers toying with a nipple—circling, pinching, rolling.

She knew she should stop him—and she also knew she wouldn't. She was vaguely aware he was reaching above her, and for a second, when the water quit pelting her, she thought he'd turned it off. But then suds frothed, gliding down her back. He'd taken the massage wand in his hand and expertly, he guided it between her legs.

"Hold me," she managed to say, her voice cracking.

"Whatever you need." He leaned back, a hand skating down her back to support her. His eyes intent, he watched her face, his own pleasure seemingly building as the hot jets soaked her. "Excellent," he murmured when a sharp cry told him he'd found her clitoris. Water swirled around the bud, making her climb.

His lips skated over her cheek, raining kisses on her skin as his passion-rough voice murmured nothings. As she arched, the hand supporting her lowered, curving over her backside. Suddenly, the water between her legs gushed, coming harder. Hotter. He'd turned up the jets.

Too much, she thought. She couldn't take this. Gasping, she felt the nozzle come so close that the metal brushed her. She wasn't sure what she felt after that. Strumming fingers. Squirting liquid. Deep probing. A hand soaped between her legs, while the nozzle washed her clean. A finger parted her, then two, and he thrust them inside.

And still she wanted more, wanted him. She needed him inside her. Hard, thick and ready, he was inches away. As her hands slid to his narrow hips, her thoughts turned as dark as the night…as dangerous as the last few days of her life. They were fracturing. Breaking into pieces.

"Come, baby," he whispered.

She convulsed.

Nothing had ever felt so good. Oliver was cooing in her ear, his rich, husky voice making her melt. His body was thoroughly aroused—she'd lost track of that for just one second—and the next thing she knew, she'd grasped his hips again, drawing him against her, wanting to feel him throb between her legs, against her flesh.

Astonished, she watched him replace the nozzle above them.

For days, she'd been running on sheer adrenaline. Was that why he'd been able to evoke this incredible passion? Was it because she was already so overstimulated? Or because she'd read his books and admired him?

And did the reasons matter? Did anyone care how lovers found each other? When his mouth found hers again, she realized she might have been satisfied, but he wasn't. His mouth had slackened, his breath quickened, his eyes had glazed. Squeezing hers shut, she kissed him back, enjoying the hard prickle of the water jet as it sprayed over her shoulders. Lowering her mouth, she skated kisses along his neck and down on his chest, until she was locking her lips over a male nipple.

"Ah…Cameron," he said simply.

Reaching down, he pushed his fingers inside her again, in a way she'd never been touched. Slowly, thoroughly, he stroked her, his fingers crooking and curving with some kind of come-hither motion she'd never felt before—at least not there. Flicking his finger, he caressed where the skin was bumpy and rippling, looking for the G-spot.

Not only did the man know what it was. He found it without trouble. And flicked. And flicked. She arched again, her gasp audible. In seconds, she was on the brink once more, meeting the greedy demands of his tongue, the sensations wrought by his slippery, velvet fingers sending her out of control. She reached down, too, her fingers wet with suds as they circled him. He was heavy with arousal and about to burst. Crying out, he flung his head back as she stroked, whispering, "You're going to make me come."

"That's the point, Oliver," she whispered back.

She brought her thumb just under the head, rubbing mind-bending circles on the underside of the shaft. Hazy darkness had dropped over her mind like a curtain. Everything was nearly black now, and she kept her eyes shut, concentrating on raw sensation. Fear had left her, replaced by the affirmation of life. By warmth. Safety. Protection.

By Oliver.

As she guided him to her, his words came on a pant, tense and urgent. "Wait a minute."

She opened her eyes then and watched him draw back the shower curtain. He reached outside long enough to get a condom he'd apparently brought into the bathroom with him. Vaguely, she wondered if Oliver always carried them, then she let the thought go—and merely stared—because he was slipping the condom over the most gorgeous piece of male equipment she'd ever laid eyes on. He was hard as a rock, straight as an arrow and ribbed in all the right places.

Her eyes drifted shut again as he edged closer, his kiss one of preparation now—a warning, a promise—before he began to push inside. For just that moment, they were strangers again. They were so alone, too. Standing in a shower, as if under the hard rain outside, the sound of water drowning out the city sounds around them. For just that moment, Peggy wondered what she was doing.

And then the moment was gone.

She knew exactly what she was doing—getting satisfaction from the hottest man she'd ever met. Her eyes opened in slits. Liquid and intense, he stared back, looking unbelievably gentle. It was his tenderness that really got to her—reaching inside and touching her heart.

She weakened then, silently damning him for looking as though he cared about her. Especially since they didn't even know each other. She damned herself, too, for letting him get this close.

Curling her fingers over his shoulders, she used her

nails to tantalize and draw him nearer. "Make love to me," she whispered simply.

"In bed?"

She was too ready. "Here."

"Fine by me."

He'd already begun moving inside her. And now he more fully entered her. She felt the quiver in his palms, the straining muscles of his thighs, the delicious shudder when he completely filled her. He was taking pleasure now, too, his movements harder, more purposeful. The shudders racking his body shook hers in turn. Ripples passed from her hips to his. Heat soared between them. He seemed to hover somewhere above her, ready to spiral down into her arms, crashing and burning. She couldn't believe the heat inside her, nor how it stroked upward in a trajectory of pleasure as his greedy tongue plundered her mouth.

And then she was there. Her breath seemed to cease. He was consuming her with sexual hunger. Thoroughly invaded, she was utterly lost to pleasure. She never wanted to return. She wanted to be with this man forever, living in the ceaseless waves of joy that were washing over her. On a cry, his hips tilted, rising sharply, and when spasms shook her, he cried again, pummeling her with fast strokes until his body went taut. Releasing, he shuddered, gasping his heartfelt satisfaction against her neck.

"Are you okay?" he whispered.

Even with the condom on, she could feel him pulsing, buried deep inside her. Okay? she wondered vaguely. It seemed an odd thing to ask, but she knew what he meant. She'd never had such satisfying sex, nor felt this grateful for a warm male body.

"Amazing," she said softly, clinging to him. She'd been so scared that she'd let herself go as never before, and now he was gazing into her eyes as if he was half in love with her.

"Yeah," she added. "I'm okay. You?"

He nodded, a smile on his lips, his dark eyes flickering over her face like a candle flame. "Oh, yeah." After a moment, he tilted his head. "I could stand here all night. But I think somebody's at the door."

Fear coiled inside her. Her lips parted in unspoken protest. Had Susan Jones followed them here? "At the door?"

"Room service."

Relief flooded her. "I forgot they were coming."

He chuckled softly, as if to remind her *she'd* been coming. "We were busy."

"Well, we'd better get out."

Angling his head downward, Oliver brushed his lips across hers. "Don't worry. I'll take care of it. Why don't you take your time and get dressed?"

Before she could respond, he'd grabbed a towel, slung it around his waist and headed for the door.

LIFTING A PIECE of turkey meat from a plate, Oliver let her take it from his fingers with her lips. She kissed his fingertips in the process. "Good, huh?" he prodded.

She tossed her head, sending a lock of hair away from her face as she dug into a dish of ice cream. "I was starved."

He sent a smile toward where she was seated cross-legged on the bed, unable to believe his good fortune over the last couple of hours. If he'd guessed any of Anna's friends could be this hot, he'd have made a date long before now. "Full?"

"Just about."

When she'd come from the bathroom wearing the black spandex pants and skimpy exercise shirt, he'd slipped his trousers back on. That was almost an hour ago. Now the nearly empty food tray lay between them. The food had been piping hot and cooked to perfection, too. Not that Oliver cared. As far as he was concerned, nothing could top that scene in the shower.

Or maybe he was wrong. Even now, he could feel more heat building between him and Cameron. They were taking comfort in each other's company, yes, but there was tension, too. Palpable, it coursed between them, manifesting in sudden sharp breaths, long sideways glances and the suggestive shift of their weight on the mattress.

Body language had always fascinated him, mostly because he needed to read it accurately while interviewing suspects. Now, watching Cameron, he decided they were about to make love again. He figured she was thinking the same.

He popped a biscuit into his mouth. "And I thought I wasn't going to get Thanksgiving dinner."

She squinted, licking her tongue around the ice-cream spoon in a way that teased his imagination. "Where do you usually go?"

"To my folks in Utah."

Despite her earlier silence, she'd been chatty during dinner, quizzing him about his interests and habits, but shying away whenever he tried to pull similar information from her. "No one special, huh?"

It was the same question Kate Olsen had asked him on the *Rise and Shine* show. "There is now."

"Touché."

He shrugged. "Really," he said, still feeling glad for the turkey feast. "I thought this was going to be my first Thanksgiving without a traditional meal. My folks decided to leave the country, and Anna...well, I guess you know about Anna."

She looked as if she didn't have a clue. "So, you like spending time with your family?"

"Yeah. You?"

He was almost sorry he'd asked. Her brown eyes turned wistful, and he could almost swear he saw them mist with tears. "Very much."

"Why aren't you with them?"

She shook her head as if to clear it of confusion, and her eyes turned sharper. "Long story."

"I'd like to hear it."

She considered a few moments, then said, "I...grew up with my mother and her sister, my Aunt Jill. She's unmarried."

Arching an eyebrow, he said, "Why does your tone lead me to believe there's story in there somewhere?"

"Because there is. A man left my aunt at the altar. He ran off with one of her attendants."

"The day of the wedding?"

She nodded. "Actually, Aunt Jill was married,"

she amended. "But only for an hour or so. Later the marriage was annulled. She'd just changed into her honeymoon clothes when she found her husband in a choir-robing room with a bridesmaid."

He frowned. "She never got over it?"

"Nope. Even worse, the bridesmaid and Aunt Jill's ex are happily married to this day. Four kids. Fortunately, they moved out of state."

"That takes the edge off," he conceded. "And your dad?"

"He left when I was a kid and started a second family."

"Ah. Another betrayal."

"We're definitely a family of women. No luck with men."

"You got lucky tonight," Oliver pointed out.

"You know what I mean."

"Did he move nearby?"

She shook her head. "No. Nearly as far as Aunt Jill's ex who went to Wyoming. Dad landed in Nebraska."

"That's not exactly a weekend jaunt from Ohio."

"No," she said. "No, it's not, Oliver."

He was sorry to see her eyes shutter, as if a transparent curtain had fallen over the irises. "Sorry," he murmured. "I didn't mean to pry. I'm just curious." He very definitely wanted to get to know a woman who made love the way she had in the shower.

"No problem. It was just hard to take. I was seven when he left, and he had two more kids."

And she'd been pushed entirely out of the picture. Oliver didn't have to ask more; he could read the

details in her eyes. He could imagine the initial promises, the long-distance phone calls, the slow-building
understanding that her daddy had really moved on,
out of her life. Oliver pushed down the flare of anger.
In his line of work, he'd heard far worse about human
behavior—real horror stories—but he hated any situation where adults couldn't happily fulfill their ob-
ligations to the kids who loved them. "You had your
mother and Aunt Jill," he reminded softly.

She nodded, warmth coming into her eyes.
"Yeah."

"And so, you're in town over the holiday because..."

"Oh," she said vaguely. "A lot of reasons."

"And Christmas?" Even as he said the words, he
felt a twinge of sadness. It really wouldn't be the
same without Anna and his folks. Next year, they'd
be together again, of course, but he kept thinking
maybe *he'd* meet someone by then.

"I'm still not sure. I might have to work—" She
offered a quick shrug as if to dispense with the topic.
"What about the rest of the holidays? Are you working?"

"Some. Anna probably told you."

"She didn't say much. You're in the FBI office
over by Grand Central, right?"

She knew he was. He'd caught her standing outside, watching him, but he decided not to mention it.
He nodded. Deciding he was finished with dinner, he
tossed aside a napkin and grabbed a champagne bottle
by the neck. "Right. But only temporarily. I live near
Quantico. More bubbly?"

"Sure."

As he poured, she continued. "What about your co-workers? Are they around during the holidays, too, or do you have to cover for them?"

It wasn't the first time she'd brought up his work life. During the earlier part of dinner, she'd encouraged him to talk about the office: who the players were. Who he liked and disliked. He'd almost wound up giving her an earful about Miles McLaughlin and Kevin Hall, but he'd thought better of it. He didn't know her that well. You never knew what might come back to haunt you.

Now he sent her a wry smile, his eyes drifting over the top she wore, his mouth drying. He took in where the tips of her breasts beaded under the fabric, looking hard, tight and ready for his mouth again. "You don't really want to talk about my work, do you?"

"Sure." Her smiles were coming more easily now, and he was surprised to find how good that made him feel. He wanted her to feel comfortable with him. "It's fascinating."

Rolling his eyes in skepticism, he leaned, settled a palm on her knee and glided it upward on her thigh. "I hate office politics."

"What about writing?"

He sighed in satisfaction, half because of the subject, half because of the slick feel of the Lycra. Beneath it, he could feel Cameron's muscles respond to his touch, leaping to life, quivering for more. "Writing's another story. I love it."

"Can you do it full-time?"

"Afraid not."

"But you're a bestseller."

"True. But they still need me at work."

"What about *your* needs?"

"Good point. Let's talk about my needs."

Her eyes fluttered. "What do you need?"

He smiled back, his eyes narrowing as he surveyed her. "What do I need?" he murmured, his voice lowering to a rasp as a hand climbed higher, toward the top of her thigh. "Now this conversation's really starting to go my way." Lifting the tray to the floor, he rolled to his belly, then scooted between her legs, preparing to push her to her back on the mattress.

She chuckled. "I was still eating."

He licked his lips playfully. "Not anymore."

"You're pretty dictatorial."

"I like hearing that," he murmured.

"What? That you're domineering and annoying?"

"You didn't say annoying."

"I'm saying it now."

"What I meant was that I like hearing you laugh."

She sent him a sideways glance, not looking convinced as he slid his hands over both thighs and upward, tracing his thumbs over her pelvic bones before molding her hips. "Really?"

"Yeah. So far, you seem pretty serious most of the time."

"I guess I am serious," she returned. "In fact, Oliver, there are a few reasons why…"

"I can fix that, you know," he murmured when her voice trailed off.

"Fix what?"

"A serious mind-set."

"I didn't know it was a problem."

"Only in certain circumstances."

"I take it this is one of those circumstances?"

"Definitely."

Her hands glided over the backs of his, and while the touch seemed meant to stop them from rising onto her rib cage, or to her breasts, Oliver felt the contact as a caress. Her lip-service reticence only made him that much more determined to have her. She'd been driving him wild since the day Anna had shown him her picture. And now she was his—in the flesh. After what had happened in the shower, there was no turning back.

Everything about her—her looks, her scent, her passion, not to mention the mysterious aura surrounding her—was driving him wilder than the picture he was still carrying in his wallet. When he glanced up from her waist, he saw that her expression had clouded. Her dark eyes appeared veiled now, as if she'd been waiting all night to divulge some special secret.

He watched in fascination as her lips twisted into a quizzical smile. "You're going to stop me from being serious?" she repeated.

"You bet."

Neither moved a muscle. But after a moment, her lips parted as if for a kiss. At the invitation, he moved his hands a fraction upward, his thumbs bracketing the indention of her navel, which he could see through the Lycra. As his long fingers curled around the fullness of her hips, he felt, rather than heard, her breath catch. It manifested in a quiver of her belly that made his thumbs vibrate. Usually he'd barely notice such a small tremor on a woman's skin, but in this particular moment—with the music playing and the lights turned down low—it rocked his world.

He was here with Cameron, a woman so gorgeous that she really could be America's Sexiest Woman. "It's just you and me," he found himself murmuring.

"Not another soul around," she agreed.

"It doesn't feel like we're strangers." He couldn't believe the passion that had erupted between them.

Again, she laughed softly. "I don't guess we are, anymore. Not exactly."

"Are you glad?"

"That this happened?" She shrugged in a way he found endearing, a lock of damp hair falling over her eye. "Yeah. I am glad. Funny, how lonely Manhattan can seem sometimes," she finished, her voice falling to a whisper.

"Eight million people can remind you that you're alone."

"I'm not alone now."

Their breaths had grown shallow, and as if by a sorcerer's magic, they were rising and falling in tandem, promising to become panting sighs. The heat of the sex they'd already shared was still warming the air, its scent permeating the room. The skin of her belly flinched beneath his touch, and once more, that tremor touched his bloodstream.

"I want you," he said, a hoarse catch in his voice.

"We really need to talk," she murmured.

"After," he promised, powerless to deny the pull of arousal. It was heady, dizzying, dragging him down. Pressing his face to her belly, he rubbed his cheeks on the Lycra. "I want you beneath me in bed."

That drew another smile from her. "Beneath?"

"Or on top."

"What about sideways?" she tested.

"Whatever."

She leaned away, grasped her shirt by the hem and simply pulled it off. She was braless, and as her breasts swung clear, he sighed. "You're full of surprises, Cameron." He couldn't wait for whatever was to happen next. He knew he'd finally met his match. Tonight was only the beginning. They were going to know each other for a very long time to come.

"Now you get the pants," she said.

Unfortunately, they were more difficult to remove, and the more he wrestled with them, the more she laughed, and the harder he got. "These are as tight as a virgin," he finally complained, frustrated when he could barely get them—and her panties—down to her midthighs.

"Payback," she murmured. "You picked out the pants, remember, Oliver?"

"Little did I know."

She squirmed. "Here. Let me help."

She wasn't helping in the least, not really. Rather, she was making a show of twisting her luscious behind to further madden him. "You show no mercy," he added under his breath.

"Poor baby," she teased.

At least the longer they played together, the more her mood lightened. Blowing out a ragged breath, he surveyed her. Never wanting a woman more, he tugged again, harder. This time, he got the pants to her knees, but suddenly lost his grip—and nearly keeled over backward.

"Patience," she warned playfully, clearly enjoying his annoyance. Her words sounded breathless and came on a giggle as she helped push the Lycra down her calves. "It's a virtue, Oliver."

"All I know about virtue," he retorted, his chuckle sounding against her cheek before he delivered a kiss, "is that soon you're not going to have any left."

"Big words," she said.

"I'm a big guy."

"You have to get my pants off first," she reminded.

"I'm determined," he assured.

"Go, tiger," she teased.

He dragged the Lycra the rest of the way down her calves, then whispered, "There."

"Good work," she commended. "Keep it up and there'll be a promotion in it for you."

"To what?"

"Love slave."

As he stripped off his own pants, he trailed his eyes upward on her long-boned thighs. They were so perfect. Hairless, creamy and smooth, he couldn't wait to feel them bracketing his hips again. Sucking in a sharp breath, he readied himself with a condom. When his eyes settled on hers again, whatever breath he'd managed to inhale squeezed from his lungs again. He could see that he'd seriously amused her by wrestling with her pants.

He said, "You think I'm funny, huh?"

"Yeah," she whispered. "I do, Oliver."

"Any other thoughts?"

"Just that tonight is…unexpected."

"Truer words were never spoken."

He propped his elbows on either side of her head, and as he continued staring deeply into her eyes, something within him stilled. All at once, the smile died on his lips. She was so good-looking. No doubt, when she walked down the street, every head turned. And he still didn't know anything about her except that she had a mother and an Aunt Jill. "I want to know more about you," he murmured.

"Such as?"

"Everything."

Her eyes had glazed under the heat of his body, and talking was obviously the last thing on her mind. "You want me to start talking right this second?"

"Later will do."

Right now, he wasn't through taking her in. Lying back on the mattress, naked, with his body molding so perfectly to hers, he trailed his eyes where her hair was drying in soft waves that looked gold in the dim light. Her eyes were soft and warm, like brown velvet. He stroked a finger down her cheek. "I don't want tonight to end. What did I do to deserve it?"

Instead of answering, she cupped long, slender fingers around his neck and urged his mouth to hers. The kiss was soft, warm and tender. Excruciatingly slow. "I'm ready," she said simply.

Time seemed to stop when he entered her. The instant he felt her slick waiting heat enveloping him, he shut his eyes and began riding into bliss. Cameron was as ready as he. Her hips met his. Her cries melded with his moans. Her kisses rained down around his shoulders.

Blackness overtook his consciousness. It was a deep, hot darkness that remained with him long after she came…long after he followed her into oblivion. It was a darkness that immediately plunged him into a deep, dreamless sleep.

GENTLY, PEGGY TUGGED a blanket around Oliver's shoulders, tucking him in, her eyes drifting over his strong bare back.

Shaking her head in consternation, she recalled how she'd rehearsed her pretty little speeches countless times. She'd known them by heart. She'd had every good intention of quickly introducing herself as Peggy Fox. Instead, she'd let Oliver think she was some woman named Cameron, not that it mattered now. There would be plenty of time to tell him about what had happened with Miles McLaughlin and Susan Jones.

Watching him, she chewed on her inner cheek, then flushed guiltily. No, she should have told Oliver immediately; she shouldn't have wasted a minute. Susan Jones was a dangerous felon, and Miles was harboring a fugitive. But how could Peggy have guessed that Oliver would wind up stepping into the shower with her? And what healthy woman would have said no to that?

Not only was Oliver handsome, brilliant and protective, but an uncanny chemistry existed between them. When it came to men, this wouldn't be the first time she'd lost her head, which was why she'd tried to swear off the opposite sex. Now she didn't want to tell Oliver the whole truth because she wanted his respect. Wouldn't it be too humiliating to tell him she'd been taken in by Miles? That she'd really believed he'd loved her?

And who was Cameron? Why would Oliver sleep with a woman he knew only by a name? As near as Peggy could tell, he thought Cameron was a friend of his sister, Anna. Peggy's usual love of a good mystery had kicked in, and now, blinking sleep from her eyes, she yawned as questions swirled through her mind.

She'd definitely botched things. But deep down, she wasn't sure she minded. In fact, she almost wished her roommates could see her now. Previously, they'd teased her when she'd gone moony-eyed while reading Oliver's books, and now she was in bed with him.

And she felt so safe. A delicious shiver claimed her as she surveyed Oliver's dark hair on the pillow. With Oliver beside her, she'd get a good night's sleep tonight. She just wished she could call her mom and Aunt Jill to say good-night. Yes, everything was going to be fine now. She pictured her and Oliver having breakfast tomorrow. Over bacon, eggs and coffee, she'd tell him…

"Maybe I'll change the story just a little," she whispered, truly not wanting him to know she'd been stupid enough to fall for Miles. And maybe if things were properly cleared up, and Miles and Susan Jones were put in jail, she could take Oliver home for Christmas to meet her mom and Aunt Jill. After all, with his folks out of the country, and Anna traveling with her boyfriend, Oliver had nowhere to go…

"Oh, Peggy," she whispered in warning.

What was happening to her resolution not to become involved? Worse, while she'd meant to get information from him about Miles, she'd wound up hearing about Oliver's personal life, leaving her with the sneaking suspicion that she'd love his sister and parents. Every gut instinct that had led her to Oliver seemed right on target. He was caring and tender, just as he seemed on TV.

As she began to slip beneath the covers and snuggle beside him, she noticed his wallet on the floor— and the edge of a condom sticking from the billfold. A smile played on her lips. *Funny,* she thought as she leaned over the bed's edge. *Hours ago I was terrified. Now I'm actually having fun.*

She flipped open the wallet, admiring his badge, then she took out the condom, placing it on the bedside table for tomorrow morning. Suddenly she frowned and slipped out a folded paper. Only a quarter of the page was visible—the paper was folded in fourths—but it was a picture of a woman. The glimpse she caught of the hair reminded her of her own.

Her throat tightened as she unfolded the picture. "It's me," she whispered, fear rushing back into her body. "Where did he get this?"

She could barely hear herself think over the blood rushing in her head. In the picture, she was wearing clothes she didn't recall wearing. Slacks and a tan cashmere sweater. Squinting, she searched her memory. Where had she worn these clothes? Had Miles photographed her in them?

"Yes," she suddenly whispered. She remembered now. For one of their early dates, she'd borrowed the top from one of her roommates, Kiki. Miles had brought along a new digital camera and he'd shot some pictures of her, saying he wanted to try it out.

Betrayal twisted inside her. The picture had been in Oliver's wallet all night. He had to have gotten the photograph from Miles. There was no other possible explanation. Only Miles had a connection to both her and Oliver.

Her eyes flew to him. He'd recognized her from this picture, but he'd kept mum. This was getting stranger by the minute. Why hadn't he said something? Pain coursed through her, then regret. Why did she have to find the picture now? After he'd made such exquisite love to her? She'd been sure she could trust him. Despite how unexpected it was, she'd even imagined they might have a future. As if a future could be built on one night's pleasure.

"What's going on?" she whispered. Had Kevin Hall also seen the picture in Oliver's possession? Was that why he'd chased her through the subway?

Well, whatever reason Oliver had for calling her Cameron, Peggy no longer wanted to know. Now it seemed possible that all three agents knew... something. Both Kevin Hall and Oliver had recognized her—and from a picture that had only been in Miles's possession. Which meant Peggy—the only witness to the relationship between Miles and Susan—could still be in danger. One last time, she stared at the picture in her hand, then she slipped from the bed. As she dressed, she began to cry silently. It was the first time she'd done so since her ordeal began.

6

"SINCE YOU WANT the results immediately, this must be a hot case, Mr. Vargo," murmured a young agent as Oliver handed over a fingerprint sample.

Hot? More like sizzling. Oliver's dream lover had disappeared into thin air nearly two weeks ago, and despite being practiced at finding suspects, Oliver hadn't been able to put his skills to use in the service of his own love life. Manhattan had never looked so big. Millions of people seemed to pass him on a daily basis—and every one of them looked like the woman he'd called Cameron…the woman who'd stolen his heart during a one-night stand. So far, he'd seen her at a news kiosk, bus stop and café, and each time, he'd given chase—only to find out he was tracking a stranger.

A phantom, he thought now. A mirage. Why had she decided to play this game of smoke and mirrors? Didn't she know he'd eventually find her?

Even worse, with Thanksgiving past, the entire city was decorated for Christmas. From inside stores, carols piped into the streets, and all along the sidewalks, trees were wrapped in white lights that twinkled like diamonds. The drizzle of November had vanished just as surely as Cameron, and now flurries were falling whimsically through the air, as if to herald the romance and magic of the season.

So, where was she? And was Cameron even her real name? Why had she left without so much as a goodbye? Hadn't the sex they'd shared affected her in the least? Or had she simply been out for a one-night stand? Did she have a boyfriend? His heart squeezed. Maybe even a husband?

Oliver had no idea what he'd do—or say—if he did find her. *When,* he silently vowed in correction. After their night together, he'd never let her get away.

"Mr. Vargo?"

Oliver returned his attention to the young agent who, in his plain brown suit and shiny black shoes looked every inch the FBI cliché. The outfit, however, thought Oliver, was preferable to the sharkskin suits favored by the agent's superiors, Miles McLaughlin and Kevin Hall. "Sorry," Oliver murmured, feeling a need to apologize, since thoughts of Cameron had made him drift. "What's your name?"

"Garrison."

"Well, Garrison, you're right," assured Oliver, staring into Garrison's bright, eager eyes. "It's…an important case to me. So, I'd appreciate it if you could run the prints now. I'd do it myself, but Miles and Kevin just called a meeting."

"An important case, huh?" echoed Garrison curiously.

"Yeah. And like I said, I could use your help." He'd gotten the prints off the black mask he'd found under the bed at the Washington Square Hotel. Quickly, he tried to push aside an image of the eyes behind it, but like everything about Cameron, those eyes still haunted him.

"I can probably have results by the time you're out of the meeting," assured Garrison. "Is this man a known felon?"

"We'll see," returned Oliver noncommittally.

"Happy to do it for you, sir." The young man's cheeks colored slightly. "I've never had a chance to say it, Mr. Vargo. But it's an honor to work with you. I've read all your books, and I'm familiar with the cases you've solved. They use your materials in a lot of our training courses, you know."

"Thanks for mentioning it. And I appreciate your running the prints." Oliver offered a nod before he headed toward his desk to grab his sports coat and tie. As he strode through the sea of gray cubicles, he blew out a sigh. Didn't Miles know he had countless better things to do than watch another demonstration of the new Quick Composite software?

Realizing the message light on his phone was blinking, he speeded his steps. Had the woman who'd called herself Cameron finally called him? Once more, he wondered how she could have left him at the hotel. At first, he'd thought something had happened to her, of course. Over the years, he'd worked enough cases that his mind always fled to the worst-case scenario. He'd imagined her being snatched from the hallway as she filled the ice bucket. Except the ice bucket was still in the room. And her duffel was missing.

The black eye mask was the only item she'd forgotten; it had gotten kicked under the bed. At least her prints had adhered to the porous material. With any luck, it would be his glass slipper—and Garrison would find a match for the print. It was a long shot, though. Cameron hadn't exactly seemed like the type to have a criminal record.

"But you never know," Oliver whispered. The woman had haunted his dreams, then materialized in the flesh, giving him sex that made all his nocturnal fantasies pale by comparison. It wasn't just the sex he missed, either. Dammit, it was the flicker of promise between them. Thoughts of her touch still made him shiver; the heat of her kisses still warmed him. Everything had seemed so special, so perfect. Like a humorous, sentimental story they'd someday tell their kids. He'd known better than to project such thoughts. And yet, that night, he'd been sure they were marking the beginning of something that might last.

And then she was gone.

Nothing that good came to an end, did it? Right now, every ringing bell, treetop angel and street-corner Santa Claus further darkened his mood; every block he walked, trying to find Cameron, only served to remind him that he was spending the holiday alone. Christmas was fast approaching, and lovers seemed to be everywhere—walking hand in hand, snuggling their cheeks against each other's coat lapels, and crooning as they took in window displays or watched the skaters in front of the tree at Rockefeller Center, their fingers clasped around bags from Tiffany's and Saks.

Grabbing his tie from the back of the chair, he

looped it around his neck as he lifted the phone receiver and checked his messages. In the second before voice mail clicked on, his heart missed a beat. His mouth dried with anticipation as he waited to hear the dreamy voice from his one night of pleasure. A slow shiver wended down his spine.

When he heard the voice mail, he whispered, ''Anna.''

Right now, Anna was second best. She could give him a lead on Cameron. Besides, it was about time she phoned. He'd been trying to reach her. He glanced over his shoulder toward a conference room, realizing if he didn't hurry, he'd be late for his meeting. Then he punched in the number Anna had left.

''Ollie?'' she said when she picked up.

''I've been trying to find you.''

Her voice sounded light and bubbly, just the way a voice was supposed to sound during an extended vacation. ''I should have let you know where I was—'' she began guiltily.

''Yeah. You should have. Mom and Dad—''

''Oh, no! Did they try to find me, too?''

''No. But they could have.''

''Sorry,'' she murmured. ''Vic and I rented a car and drove all over the islands. Then we wound up stopping in this quaint little village and decided to stay. Oh, Ollie, I wish you could see it! I wish you were here! It's so incredibly romantic!''

''Romantic's the last thing I need,'' he muttered.

Her voice dropped. ''I don't know, but I think Vic's going to ask me to marry him. He's got this look in his eyes—''

That much had been obvious for the past year. "Again?"

If memory served Oliver correctly, Vic had asked before.

"Oh, this is so different," assured Anna. "This time I might say yes. All those other times, I wasn't sure. But now…"

Shoving aside the misgivings about his own love life, Oliver congratulated her. But what he most wanted to know about his future brother-in-law was whether he'd helped Anna put Cameron's picture into the computer. Was the woman really a friend of theirs as he'd assumed? Before he could ask, Anna plunged into a conversation about their parents, whom he'd spoken to on the phone, and then she wanted to know how Oliver was feeling, since he had to fend for himself over Christmas. "Vic and I feel so guilty, leaving you by your lonesome, Big Brother," she finished.

"Speaking of my being alone," he said, circling back to his topic. "I want to know about Cameron." He wedged the phone more tightly between his jaw and shoulder, glancing once more toward the conference room. Wincing, he realized that Agent Garrison was motioning to him, since the meeting was starting. He waved. *Be right there,* he mouthed.

"Uh…Cameron?" Anna asked.

"Yeah," he managed to say on a frustrated sigh. "Look, I've only got a minute. I've got a meeting. But I called the Sex Files when I couldn't reach you, Anna. They swore there's no one employed there by that name. In case they were covering for you, I went over there."

"You went to my office?"

"Yeah." He'd walked the place like a crime grid, going methodically from floor to floor. "I didn't see her."

Anna was starting to sound concerned. "See who? Ollie, what are you talking about?"

"I'm talking about Cameron."

"Cameron? You'll have to backtrack. You lost me somewhere—"

To make matters worse, Anna suddenly giggled, and Oliver suspected that Vic was tickling her toes or some such. "Anna," he warned.

"Oliver, what are you talking about?" she repeated.

"As if you don't know."

"I don't."

Yeah, right. Memories of the night came flooding back, and he felt bands tightening around his chest. Suddenly, he was standing at the parade again, his hips locking with Cameron's. Her back was pressed against the police barricade, her hips arching in a way that held countless promises. Then he saw himself drawing back the shower curtain and gliding his hands around her waist as he stepped under the hot-water jets. Later, she'd looked so beautiful, laughing as he tugged off those ridiculously tight Lycra pants she'd worn for his benefit. Suddenly, his throat felt raw.

It had been the best night of his life.

He recalled awakening, too, with early-morning light seeping through a crack in the curtain. He'd been disoriented for the first moment, the mattress and pillow not feeling like his own, nor like the bedding from the countless hotels where he'd stayed this past year, nor like Anna's. Then he'd smiled and reached for her, whispering, "Cameron."

But she was gone.

He shook his head in frustration. "Anna," he said, "you know what I'm talking about." In case she wanted to play games, he plunged into his side of the story, beginning with when she'd come to his office and crossed the Sex Files with the Quick Composite software. "Did Vic help you with this?" he finished.

"No. And really, Oliver," she said. "This wasn't a prank. I don't have any girlfriends named Cameron. And I've never seen the woman in that picture."

The worst thing was, he believed her. "You're sure, Anna?"

"Positive."

His heart sank. Besides the fingerprints, Anna had been his only real lead. "Then how did this happen?" he said.

"Who knows?" said Anna half seriously. "Maybe she really did materialize from a picture. Maybe the image of America's Sexiest Woman was really created from thin air. This is Christmas. The season for miracles."

Being so hopelessly in love with Vic was obviously clouding his sister's common sense. "As if you believe in magic."

"Well, no. But nothing else makes sense." She added, "Is there someone else who might have played a prank?"

"No. Only you." He sighed. "I've got to go. The

meeting's starting. It's another demonstration of Quick Composite."

"Sorry, Big Brother. I know that's the bane of your existence."

That, and the missing Cameron. He couldn't believe that he'd lost her...maybe forever. After hanging up, he headed toward the conference room. Sure enough, everyone was assembled, the seats were all taken, and the demonstration was in full swing. Leaning against a wall near a Christmas tree, Oliver let his mind stray, focusing his attention at the spot in front of Grand Central where Cameron had previously stood watching him. His heart lurched as if she might really appear, as if he really might see her again.

But he didn't. It could have been a scene in a snow globe, with shoppers carrying brightly wrapped packages as they rushed along Forty-second Street. The snow was coming down harder, the swirling flakes as thick and white as cotton. Unbelievable, he thought. How could Cameron have vanished? And who on earth was she—if she wasn't Anna's friend?

With difficulty, Oliver forced his attention on the meeting, his eyes settling on Miles who was standing at the front of the room beside a television monitor. The birthmark that stained his left cheek was somehow compelling, as were intense blue eyes that sparked with too much intelligence. Oliver had been around the office long enough to know Miles was a ladies' man, and he thought it was a shame. Too many women were easily drawn in by power-obsessed men who liked to be in control.

"What Kevin and I most wanted to show the

group,'' Miles was saying, pushing his hands deeply into the pockets of finely woven gray wool slacks, ''is how this software works. It shows us how suspects on our Most Wanted list will look while wearing various disguises.

''We've had similar software, of course, but never anything as accurate as this. Let's take…'' Miles nodded at Kevin. ''Not a top-ten criminal from VICAP, but someone less important. Let's say a bank robber. This suspect's slated to be on one of the new updated wanted posters. If we're lucky, we may even get one of the true-crime television shows—maybe *To Catch A Thief*—to run her picture.''

Miles nodded at Kevin, who hit the remote control button. A picture blinked onto the screen, causing Oliver to nearly choke.

Impossible, he thought, feeling stunned. It was Cameron!

The image of his dream lover, the woman who'd haunted his mind for weeks, filled the screen. The same picture was still folded in his wallet; he'd shown it to the desk clerk at the Washington Square Hotel two weeks ago, and he'd been able to confirm that she'd registered under a phony name. Somehow Oliver managed not to react as his eyes took in the picture on the screen.

''As you can see,'' Miles was saying, ''this is Susan Jones. Aka Sharon Smith. We know she's somewhere in New York City. Or at least she was. Kevin chased her through one of the subways a couple weeks ago.''

Oliver's lips parted as he took in the information.

The woman was on the run—and she'd known it while she was making love to him in the Washington Square Hotel.

"She's got a rap sheet a mile long," assured Kevin.

Feeling sick, Oliver realized what must have happened. While Anna had been crossing the Sex Files and Quick Composite software, Oliver had also been working with the Wanted list. Anna said they could minimize that and work in another window, but she'd goofed somehow and accidentally printed Susan Jones's picture.

He shook his head. This still made no sense and yet there had to be a reasonable explanation. Why had Susan Jones appeared in his life at exactly the same time that Anna accidentally printed her picture from the Wanted list? It seemed...uncanny. Too coincidental. Did all this mean that she'd been watching him? But why? And why had she slept with him?

Somehow, Oliver made it through the next few minutes, watching in utter stupefaction as the lover he'd been aching for was further exposed as a criminal, and displayed as a blonde, then a brunette. It seemed an eternity before he could leave the meeting. When he did, anxious to get to his office where he could be alone, Agent Garrison pulled him aside, handing him the results of the fingerprint analysis and the rap sheet. "Sir," he said, "are you okay? You look like you've seen the Ghost of Christmas Past."

Oliver had. His eyes raked down the rap sheet. Susan Jones had gotten her start in juvenile detentions, and what followed was the standard history of bad male partners and petty thefts, all of which led to a series of bank robberies. Imprisoned once, she'd been out on parole when she robbed another bank. Now she was on the run with three million from a heist.

"She's on the Wanted list," he said softly.

And even worse, Oliver still wanted *her*.

IT TOOK ANOTHER WEEK of Oliver employing all his tracking skills to find her again. He was standing outside the West Fourth Street station where he'd previously spotted her, stamping snow from his feet, trying to keep them from going numb. The way he figured it, Susan Jones had recognized him from TV, known he was an agent and decided to have a little fun with him.

He had no other way of understanding what had happened. Still, it seemed unlikely that she'd start following him at the same time that Anna accidentally accessed the Most Wanted list and printed her picture. Well, whatever had happened, Oliver knew there was a logical explanation. One he intended to find. The bottom line was that she'd seduced him....

It had worked, too. He'd half fallen in love with her. Now he'd been on her tail for days, running just a step behind her. He'd found hotels all over the city where she'd stayed, and now he'd returned to the subway station where he'd seen her; he'd been staking it out every day for the past week.

Which was why he wasn't surprised when she appeared.

"About time," he whispered, watching her exit the subway. While she walked, she resituated the duffel, moving the strap from one shoulder to the other. As he thought about all the lacy lingerie inside, his lips thinned into a grim line.

"Don't let her get to you," he muttered.

All day, she'd felt so close he could almost taste her. As she turned right, heading toward Bleeker Street, he followed. She made a right onto Bleeker, walking alongside a string of bakeries and toward electronic stores on the corner of Seventh Avenue. She was outside a place called Zito's when he caught up to her, grabbed her arm from behind and swung her around.

He damned his heart for missing a beat. But she was more beautiful now than ever. Heavy snow was falling, catching in blond hair as the wind whipped it across her reddened cheeks. Her mouth was pursed in surprise, but she looked ready to be kissed. Scents of hot, fresh-baked bread poured onto the street surrounding them.

"It's you," she said on a sharp intake of breath.

"Surprised?" Before he could think it through, he angled his head down, his mouth stopping just a fraction from hers, so close he could feel the warmth of her breath and smell its mint scent. A sudden, visceral need for her made his nostrils flare. In his mind's eye, he was pulling her downward, into the street, plundering her mouth with his. For a second, he felt so blinded by passion that he didn't even see her. Forget hauling her in, he thought. He'd die if he didn't make love to her again.

"How did you know where I was?" she whispered.

"Luck," he returned gruffly, and because it wasn't strictly true, he added, "Years of training." Seeing her had wrenched him out of his senses; only now could he feel the cold he'd been fighting for hours as it seeped into the coat he'd haphazardly buttoned.

"You've been looking for me?"

Dogging her every move for days, he thought. He'd taken off work so he could tirelessly pound the pavement. "Sure. Just like every other agent in the city."

She looked afraid. "Every agent? Why? What are you going to do?"

Did she really think a little sex would persuade him to ignore his vows to the law? His voice was deceptively soft. "Haul you in."

She swallowed hard. He could see her throat working, and the fast tick of pulse beneath her smooth skin as he drew her an inch closer. Suddenly, he wasn't quite so sure of his intentions. Not when her mouth was so irresistibly close, and when strands of her hair were teasing whisker-roughened cheeks he hadn't bothered to shave. He hadn't had time. Ever since the meeting with Miles where she'd been identified as a criminal, thoughts of her had consumed him.

Silently, he cursed the moment he'd ever laid eyes on her. He could almost believe he hated her. This whole series of events seemed so crazy. So unreal. The next thing he knew, people would probably be calling him Virtual Oliver. Or E-Oliver. How could he have slept with a felon?

"I got your fingerprints off the mask," he felt oddly compelled to explain.

"My fingerprints? Why would you want my fingerprints?"

"Quit playing naive with me." Once more, he

damned her for looking so innocent. Frightened even. She was staring up at him. Those brown eyes were riveted to his face, seeming to plead with him. "Stop it," he muttered.

"What?"

Staring with those eyes that hooked into him and wouldn't let go. Feeling oddly helpless, he tightened his grip and pulled her closer. Her chest brushed his. Through her coat, he felt the cushion of her breasts, the hard, erect nipples. Electricity zipped through him at the contact, and heat spread through his lower belly. Because her green raincoat was too lightweight for the weather, he imagined taking it off her. Like before, in the Washington Square Hotel, she'd be standing there with wet, tight clothes he could see through. Before he knew it, he was thinking of the panties she'd worn that night. Tight and black, they'd barely covered her.

He took a steadying breath, but it was no use. His heart thudded dully, and every time he pushed aside his errant thoughts, more raced back. Still, he was determined not to let her get to him. Watching her, he told himself he didn't give a damn about the lightweight coat—or if the woman died from pneumonia because she was wearing it.

"I've never been fingerprinted." She looked stricken, and her teeth chattered through the words. "You have to let me talk to you. You're right. I was following you, Mr. Vargo."

Mr. Vargo. She'd reverted to that again. A harsh chuckle erupted from his lips. "After what you did to me in that hotel room, why don't you call me Oliver?''

"What I *did* to you?"

He jerked her closer, the movement so abrupt that their hips slammed. He felt the cushion of her belly now, the hard ridges of her pelvic bones. "You didn't just follow me," he muttered, the raw huskiness in his voice belying the tone. "You seduced me. You made me want you."

"You want me?"

More than life. He could feel every bit of her pressing down the front of him. The wall of his chest had molded to her curves. No doubt she could feel him, too—every hard, hot, blessed inch. "What do you think?" he returned in a near growl. As close as they were, she could surely feel the evidence of how much he needed her.

"I had to talk to you," she repeated, her voice lowering so he barely heard the soft catch in her throat. "I had to tell you something."

Vaguely, he wondered what this woman had done to him. She was a criminal, but he could barely attend to her words. As she talked, his eyes had fastened to her mouth. It was so red. So ripe. He was remembering the taste of it soaked with champagne, and how glad he'd felt to share a Thanksgiving dinner with someone. And now it was almost Christmas. Farther up the street, near the electronics store, a red-suited Santa had begun ringing a bell and collecting for the Salvation Army.

"But you didn't do much talking." Oliver forced himself to say. "Did you?"

Her wary brown eyes skated guiltily sideways as if she was about to make a run for it. When they returned to his, their expression had grown harder, the irises darkening and gaining a steely determination. "No," she admitted. "No, I didn't. I was scared and I'd been so alone, and so I—"

"Wanted a little male comfort?"

He could see from the set of her jaw that the woman had more strength in her than she'd previously shown, but he should have known that. After all, she'd robbed banks. "Something like that," she muttered. "And," she added, "you didn't mind giving it."

"No," he admitted.

And judging from her sudden, audible inhalation she, too, was still thinking of the night they'd spent together. As his jaw slackened, he felt cold air race inside his mouth, drying it. Needing something wet and hot, he was sorely tempted to kiss her. He wanted one more taste—just one—before he took this woman in for questioning. If the truth be told, he wanted more than a simple kiss.

But he was too much of a lawman. "You had your chance to talk."

"Not really," she defended, her lips still only a hairbreadth away. "You're the one who stepped into the shower."

His eyes pierced into hers, and while he fought it, he knew she saw the dark dancing lights of desire. For a fleeting second, they shared the memory of exactly how they'd spent their time. He was touching her intimately, sudsing between her legs. "That I did."

"You had a picture of me," she said, her eyes returning to his, her voice sounding weak before it was whisked away by the wind. "Where did you get it?"

"Out of the FBI computer system."

She gasped. "That's impossible!"

"Why?"

"I haven't done anything wrong!"

"You're a felon," he said, "and I'm taking you in." Suddenly, he realized his mouth was nearly on hers. It hovered mere inches from her lips. How had it gotten so close? His parted in surprise—or for the kiss. For a second he was lost. "I'm taking you in," he repeated, this time to convince himself. And then, before he thought it through, he added, "But not before we get something straight."

"What?"

"This, Cameron," he muttered. "Or Susan. Or whoever you are."

Oliver's mouth gave no warning. It crashed down on hers in an assault that wasn't quite a kiss, after all. It was more a command, and the undammed flood of his suppressed need. It wasn't the least bit polite, either. He moved his mouth on hers, plunging his tongue as he thrust a hand behind her neck, up into all that gorgeous, silken hair he'd been sure he'd never touch again. Not bothering to hide his moan of satisfaction, he plunged his tongue deeper for a kiss that carried no trace of the gentleman. The kiss didn't have to. This woman was the worst kind of criminal.

And she was kissing him back.

It was so heavenly that Oliver understood why women swooned. Moments ago, he'd sworn he was too much of a lawman to sink to this level. But now he knew differently. With every push of her silken tongue, the woman was dragging him down farther. He was drowning in heat. He wanted to take her home and put her in bed. He wanted to drive his throbbing aroused flesh so deep inside her that she wouldn't know where he ended and she began. Despite the snow falling all around them, he was boiling.

Suddenly, she wrenched. "Stop." She gasped.

He wasn't ready to, but she was right. They had no business fulfilling their physical appetites, regardless of the magnetic pull between them. He leaned back enough to see her face. By the minute, she looked more appealing. Her eyes appeared dazed with passion. Her expression was vaguely confused, as if she wasn't quite sure what had just happened.

He shared the feeling. He'd meant to take her straight to FBI headquarters. Instead, his gaze had fixed to the red bud of her mouth again, and he was standing here like a fool—as if he had all night to watch snowflakes melt on her tongue.

"Let me go," she repeated.

Instinctively, his grasp loosened. It was as though every bit of information in his considerable repertoire that concerned apprehending suspects simply vanished from his mind. That hot little mouth he'd just kissed had said, *Let me go.* And like a person mesmerized, he'd simply complied. In the one-second window before he realized his mistake and reached for her again, she seized the advantage, turned and bolted.

Under his breath, he cursed softly, knowing as he swung out a hand that it was too late. He missed the sleeve of her coat by a fraction. Grinding his heel to the pavement, he started to run, but he hit a patch of ice and slipped. He didn't fall, but the near spill gave her a head start.

"Wait," he muttered, knowing she never would.

And then he took off after her.

7

"C'MON," Peggy muttered, trying to ignore the icy, burning air knifing to her lungs, not to mention the pleasantly bruised, swollen feeling of her mouth where Oliver had kissed her. Just thinking of his greedy tongue diving between her lips sent spears of heat shooting to her core. It was the wrong time for unwanted memories from the Washington Square Hotel to come racing back, but she could so easily imagine Oliver the way she'd left him, sleeping like an angel—her Avenging Angel, she'd thought—with his dark hair curling on the pillow...

Well, he was no angel now.

And she'd been right to leave that night. Her picture had been in his wallet. And what had he meant by saying she was a felon? And why had he called her Susan? He was chasing her, acting as if his colleague Kevin Hall...

"Susan," she whispered, fear and the exertion of running warming Peggy's body. It was definitely a name Peggy didn't want to contemplate. Surely, he couldn't have been referring to Susan Jones...and yet that was the only other Susan preying on Peggy's mind. Had Oliver connected the two of them somehow? She had no idea what was going on—only that he'd have to have some connection with Miles to get her picture.

Run, she thought, dodging shoppers on the sidewalk. Down a side street was a tree lot where men were selling trees and rope pine, and she nearly plowed into a young couple carrying a spruce. Just as narrowly, she missed a red-suited man ringing a bell for the Salvation Army, and her heart suddenly ached at the bizarre turn this holiday season had taken.

At least Oliver hadn't caught her. Just as she'd taken off, she'd heard a *whoof* behind her. Maybe he'd fallen. Good. That would buy her some extra time.

The duffel was so heavy, though, and she was freezing, her side aching. Realizing the bag was slowing her down, she shifted it from one shoulder to the other, now fighting to keep her forward momentum while the swinging weight of the bag threatened to whirl her around. Vaguely, she wondered what wrong turn she'd made in her life. How had all this happened? By this age, just like her mom and Aunt Jill, Peggy had thought she'd be settled into a safe, happy life somewhere, maybe even back in Ohio. Instead, she was…

Run! Her mind commanded. *Run, Peggy!* Her feet pounding harder on the pavement, she could only pray she wouldn't hit a patch of ice, but the snow was wet, and the temperature so low that the sidewalks had frozen. *Faster!* she thought. *Do you want to get caught?*

Hadn't she heard Oliver say he meant to haul her in?

Did he mean arrest me? For what? She couldn't
risk any vulnerability where Miles McLaughlin was
concerned. Oliver might take her to jail, he might
even kiss her until every inch of her insides felt pum-
meled and mushy—but Susan Jones would kill her.
Maybe Miles McLaughlin would, too, since she'd
seen the money in the suitcase.

"Get me out of here," she whispered.

Ahead, a string of Yellow Cabs were riding
bumper-to-bumper on Seventh Avenue. All she had
to do was hail one. In the periphery of her vision, she
saw stacks of equipment in the plate-glass windows
of some electronics stores—TVs, VCRs and DVD
players. In one more minute, she'd be on the avenue.
One more after that, and she'd be inside a warm taxi.

Suddenly, he grabbed her.

Just as before, he'd taken her from behind. Gasping, she tried to keep going, dragging him with her,
hoping he'd lose his grip and let go.

No such luck. Once more, he spun her around. As
her heels slid on the ice, she felt herself spiraling like
a child's top. She was nose-to-nose with his handsome face when she skidded to a stop. Her body was
flush with his, and although she tried to stifle the traitorous responses, sensations went wild inside her.
Bullets of awareness ricocheted. Excitement hitched.
Her core melted. Suddenly, she felt so hot that it
could have been a sunny day in the Caribbean, and
she hated him for it.

"What do you want?" she muttered. As she spoke,
the wave of heat inside her crested and fell. Cold

rushed back into her with an icy blast of winter wind, and her ungloved fingers suddenly felt like icicles.

"You."

The unexpected comment took her breath. Yes, moments ago, in his eyes, she'd seen how much. Now male awareness was still in the dark gaze that surveyed her. Black, wavy hair was thrust back from a high forehead, accentuating those edgy, alert, questioning eyes that brimmed with equal parts lust and intelligence. Yes, ever since their sensual night together, he'd been as haunted as she.

"You want to take me to jail," she countered. "Isn't that what you said?"

"Why shouldn't I?"

"Because I didn't do anything wrong. What's going on here? Why are you chasing me?"

"Because you ran," he returned, his voice deceptively mild.

"But you said you were taking me in. Let me go," she begged, still reeling from the kiss and feeling terrified that he'd try to take her to the FBI office. "Please. If that night meant anything to you at all…"

The hardness in his eyes relaxed a fraction, and he looked torn. "You said you had something to say to me."

At least that was something. Panicked, she glanced around and found herself staring into the bank of televisions in the store window. Should she try to ask for help? Or was she setting herself up for another betrayal? What was his relationship with Miles and how had he gotten the picture?

After she'd found it tucked inside his wallet, she'd

considered leaving town. What else could she do? She figured if she vanished awhile, things would be fine. Only the thought of having to explain her situation to her mom and Aunt Jill had stopped her from leaving New York. If they knew what had happened, they'd be as worried as she. It wasn't every day that she caught an FBI agent—much less, one she was engaged to—in bed with a felon. Or with money that was probably from a bank heist. And then she'd nearly gotten shot.

"Where did you get that picture in your wallet?" she demanded again, registering the desperation in her own voice. "The one of me."

"Like I said, from the computer at work. Quit playing games."

"I'm not playing games. I'm running for my life."

Slowly, he loosened his fingers, lightening his grip on her arm. Surprised, she started to edge backward—then thought better of it. If she bolted again, Oliver might chase her, and next time, he might not be this forgiving.

She watched as he reached into the pocket of his dark wool coat, pulled out a piece of paper, unfolded it against his chest, then held it up for her to read. She shivered as her eyes skated over another picture of herself. It was the same one she'd found in Oliver's wallet. But now, below it was a rap sheet she recognized as belonging to Susan Jones. Her eyes ran down the facts, taking in the list of juvenile detention homes, then the bank heists. For a second, she could swear she was only imagining this. But no. Her picture was associated with the other woman's crimes, and her mind could barely begin to take in the implications.

"This is impossible," she whispered, dread washing over her. She was a good person. How had her picture become attached to a list of crimes?

"What's impossible?" he queried.

Her lips parted in astonishment, and she became aware that her heart was beating too hard, banging against her ribs. "Miles," she murmured. Could he have done this?

"Miles?"

"I'm not Susan Jones," she managed to say, her mind reeling. "You know that, don't you?"

"Ah," he returned, not looking the least bit convinced. "I guess you're Cameron then. Or Sharon Smith? Or some other alias?"

The implications were still sinking in. "That's my picture," she continued, wondering what—if anything—would convince him of the truth. "But I've never committed any crimes." She was the kind of person who firmly shut sidewalk newspaper bins when she found them open, just so people wouldn't walk off with free newspapers. And yet the FBI thought she was a bank robber. Her mind was racing. No wonder she'd been chased through the subway. "That black man, the man you work with—"

"Kevin Hall."

"He chased me through the subway. He must have thought I was Susan Jones."

"Yeah. He did." Oliver's eyes had gone watchful, as if he expected nothing but the worst. "He still does. And so do I."

"If you think I'm Susan Jones, why'd you sleep with me! What kind of man are you? I was trying to get help—"

"Hardly what you did." He chuckled, but the soft laughter didn't meet his eyes. "And at the time, if you must know, I thought you were someone else."

"I *am* someone else!" she insisted.

"No doubt you're someone else every day of the week."

"After…after…"

When her voice trailed off, she tried to tell herself that the mad tick of pulse in her throat was due to how fast she'd been running, not to his nearness. But it was a lie. The warmth of his breath was mixing with hers, both were fogging the air, and in that instant, Peggy wanted nothing more than to feel his mouth close down on hers again with hungry heat.

"Yes?" he prodded.

Swallowing around the lump lodging in her throat, she fought the helpless panic threatening to overwhelm her. "After what happened at the hotel, I'd expect you to at least give me the benefit of the doubt."

"What happened at the hotel is that you left me," he said, his gaze drifting over her face and settling briefly on her lips before rising to her eyes again. "High and dry."

"If you'll just let me get into my duffel," she returned, "I've got an ID card. I can prove who I am. This all started because I used to amuse myself by reading true-crime books and mysteries. I also read the Wanted posters at the airport—" Inhaling sharply, she prepared to plunge on, no longer caring what he thought. "I'm a flight attendant," she explained. In fact, it had been on a New York–London flight that she'd met Miles McLaughlin. Soon after, they'd begun dating.

Tilting his head as if he didn't believe a word, he said, "Go on."

"My name's Peggy," she said. "Peggy Fox." That, at least felt good to her. Almost as good as if she'd said, *The name's Bond. James Bond.*

"Pleased to meet you," Oliver said dryly.

She managed a nod. "Same here."

He merely jerked her closer. "If you're not Susan Jones, then how did your picture get into the FBI's computer? And why didn't you bother to correct me when I called you Cameron?"

"Why *did* you call me Cameron?"

"Answer my question first."

"Because…" Her heart hammered, but she was too embarrassed to tell him the truth. When she'd met him at the parade, she'd intended to tell him the truth—the whole truth. But once Oliver had opened the shower curtain and stepped inside, all rational thought had fled. After that, she'd wanted to hide her misjudgment regarding Miles. Then she'd found her picture in his wallet—and fled. Now, once more, she wondered what he'd think if he knew how gullible she was? No. Truly, it was too humiliating to tell a man as sexy and competent as Oliver Vargo that other men had taken advantage of her. "Well, that night," she said, "when you got into the shower with me, I

didn't want you to stop…to stop…uh, you know…"
That much was the truth.

The flash of heat in his eyes said he understood.

Still, this wasn't going as she'd hoped. Every pretty
speech she'd rehearsed had vanished. It was as if
someone had opened a file drawer inside her mind
and whipped out all the pertinent files. "As I said,
I'm a crime buff. In fact, I've read your books." Despite the bad timing, she added, "I really like them."

He eyed her a long moment. "I see. You're a book
critic, too. Which airline?"

She quickly named it. "But I'm on suspension
right now." She sighed. "And I really do work for
the airline, I swear. You can check it out. I live downtown with four other flight attendants. The apartment's only got one bedroom, but since we're usually
in the air at the same time, the arrangement works
out fine. And there's a couch."

Realizing she was getting breathless, she tried to
slow the pace of her words, but a floodgate had
opened. Maybe this nightmare was coming to an end.
Maybe Oliver really would help her. Maybe there was
a reasonable explanation for how he'd wound up carrying her picture in his wallet. *The same picture that's
attached to a rap sheet,* she thought with a sinking
heart. If only he'd listen…

"Please hear me out," she rushed on. "A few
weeks ago there was a boy seated in coach who had
to go to the bathroom. But an awful lady from first-
class pitched a fit and wouldn't let him use the lav
up front. I got mad and told her off…" Color flooded
Peggy's cheeks. "Usually, I wouldn't have lost my

temper that way. I'm great with travelers and always get high marks on reviews for having good people skills…''

"But you got angry because…"

She'd had a tiff with Miles. They'd dated three months, and had just gotten engaged, and yet Peggy felt he'd seemed distant. Boy, was her radar off. Distant was an understatement, as she found out that evening, when she'd caught him in bed with Susan Jones.

For the first time in weeks, images Peggy had held at bay came rushing back. Feeling mortified, she remembered herself on one of their last dates. She'd been hanging on to Miles's arm as they entered the Rainbow Room, grinning up at him, gushing with happiness. She'd combed the city—searching everywhere from Bloomingdale's to Bergdorf Goodman's—for the simple black dress she'd worn that night. Everything had to be perfect because she suspected he was going to propose. Three months of whirlwind dating had taken her to a dream come true.

She was hardly surprised when she'd found the engagement ring floating in a flute of champagne. Only two days later, after she'd gotten suspended, Peggy had gone straight to Miles's Upper West Side town house, hoping to surprise him—and that's when she'd caught him in bed with Susan Jones, a felon she'd immediately recognized from the Wanted posters at the airport.

Of all people.

Once more, Peggy heard the woman say, "What's she doing here?" And then, as if in slow motion, Susan rolled over on the mattress, lifted a revolver from the bedside table, aimed it and fired as Miles jumped out of bed, naked. Later, Peggy had imagined Miles dressing and running outside. No doubt he'd flashed his badge, telling worried neighbors that he'd checked things out and the shooter was gone. Maybe he'd even said that he'd accidentally discharged his own weapon inside the house. Heaven only knew what lies he'd come up with.

Heat deepened in her cheeks as crimson color continued flooding her skin. No, she'd never divulge her personal relationship with Miles to anyone, least of all Oliver Vargo. For weeks, she'd pushed aside every thought of the event. Now, something steely coiled inside her as she surveyed Oliver. Despite their night together, she'd never let him get under her skin. She was through with men. When it came to them, she had a blind spot and couldn't anticipate betrayal. Even if Oliver helped her now, that was no proof that he'd be different in the long run.

"Because…" he repeated.

She settled for saying, "I was in a bad mood."

"I see."

He didn't, of course, but she nodded, anyway, suppressing a shiver. Had Miles really tampered with FBI computer files, attaching her picture to Susan Jones's rap sheet? "Unbelievable," she muttered under her breath. "Anyway," she continued, raising her voice, "what I'm trying to get at is that I saw—and recognized Susan Jones."

He stared at her in disbelief. "Let me get this straight. You, Susan Jones, *saw* Susan Jones?"

If he really thought she was Susan Jones, this

would sound awfully strange. For the first time, she noticed the pallor of his skin, and the snowflakes catching in his eyelashes and realized Oliver was as cold as she. Nodding, she said, "Yes. And like I said, I'm not Susan Jones."

He merely nodded. "And then?"

Here was the tricky part. For a moment, looking into eyes that did seem to soften as she told her story, she suddenly considered telling him the whole truth, but she simply couldn't, not after the way he'd made love to her in the hotel. She felt she'd die of mortification if he knew the truth about her and Miles. "I was an attendant on a Los Angeles–New York flight," she lied, starting over again, wishing she wasn't so nervous, so the facts would come out in a straightforward, coherent way. But how could a woman be coherent when she'd been shot at? She took a deep breath. "It was during the fight in first-class—when I let the little boy use the lav—that I saw Susan Jones and Miles McLaughlin. Together."

Better to say that than admit she'd found them in the bedroom, or that the argument over the little boy was the precursor to her getting suspended from work, which in turn led her to Miles's front door, which was where the encounter really took place. She took another deep breath. Confronting Oliver like this was bad enough, but it was better than telling him about her failed love life.

"Miles McLaughlin?" he said. "The FBI agent? How do you know him?"

"I don't," she lied again, determined to hide her mortification at how easily she'd been taken in by the man. "But flight attendants are always informed when law enforcement officers come on board. So, I knew his name and that he worked for your agency." Pleased at how credible she was starting to sound, she blew out a shaky sigh of relief. She wasn't really lying, either. The gist of what she'd said was true.

"You saw a federal agent I work with in the company of Susan Jones?"

She nodded. "I recognized her from a Wanted poster." That was true, too.

"Hmm," he said simply.

"Susan Jones had a different hair color and style," she clarified, "so most people probably wouldn't have recognized her."

"But you're a crime buff," he repeated. "So you did?"

"Yes. I pay close attention. Miles…er, Mr. McLaughlin…was seated in first-class with her. They were a *couple*." She wondered how much plainer she should make this without telling Oliver she'd caught Miles in bed with the woman. Or that she and Miles had been engaged.

"A couple?"

She managed another nod, starting to feel as ridiculous as she was cold. "Yes. They were…*kissing*."

Right now, kissing was the last thing she wanted to discuss with Oliver. Only five minutes ago his firm mouth had been latched to hers. Even now, her lips were still tingling.

"Why didn't you call the police?"

Finally, she thought, a reasonable question. "I would have," she returned. "But I didn't recognize the woman immediately. While we were airborne, I kept staring at her. When she noticed the attention, I even asked her if we'd met before. She said no, but something about her kept niggling, and I couldn't let it go.''

''And then…''

''After we deplaned, I followed her into the parking lot at LaGuardia, trying to place her.''

''And?''

''That's where she tried to shoot me.''

His lips parted in disbelief.

''She really did try to shoot me,'' Peggy insisted, the scene replaying. He seemed to see something in her eyes that gave him pause. Maybe she'd been able to convince him there was some reasonable thread that held her story together. ''I've been on the run ever since.''

''The more you talk, the stranger your story gets.''

Sudden tears stung her eyes. ''I know, but you have to believe me.''

He arched an eyebrow. ''No one heard the shot?''

That did seem unlikely. She shook her head. ''Maybe the gun had a silencer,'' she explained. Actually, the report had been ear-splitting and had probably drawn the attention of neighbors. Wishing Oliver wasn't such a stickler for details, she chewed her lower lip. ''Look, I don't know. I saw the gun…but, uh, I don't remember hearing anything. And anyway, the parking lot was totally deserted.''

''At the airport?''

She nodded. ''LaGuardia is huge.'' Fragments of the speeches she'd spent so much time rehearsing were starting to come back to her now. "Foolishly," she raced on, now speaking her practiced lines, "I said something to them. Mr. McLaughlin was still with her, of course." She paused, thinking fast. "They were leaving the airport together in an old, refurbished Jaguar."

Oliver's ears pricked up at that. Obviously he'd seen or heard of the Jag. It was Miles's pride and joy. "What color was the car?"

Feeling relieved, she said, "White."

Seeing how thoughtful Oliver looked, she felt another wave of hope. "Can you remember any other details?" he asked.

"It's got red upholstery. And it was in the back seat that I saw the money."

"Money?"

She nodded. "In a black suitcase in the back seat. It…was partially open, and I saw a hint of green. I think it was the money she took from the bank she robbed." Again, that much was the truth.

He looked skeptical. "Exactly how much is a hint?"

Closing her eyes, Peggy tried to remember. "Not much," she admitted. "I mean, this wasn't an open suitcase with neatly stacked rows of dollars. I only saw the corners of a handful of bills. It looked like they were stuffed into the case."

"So, you're not sure if the suitcase was really *full* of money?"

She had to shake her head. "No. I guess not."

"But you're sure the woman was Susan Jones?"

"Yes," she returned quickly. "There have to be

pictures of her at your office. You'll see that she and I really aren't the same person. Here——'' She reached for the zipper to the duffel, but then realized if she opened the overstuffed bag now, the risqué clothes would fall onto the sidewalk. ''If we could just sit down, I can show you my ID. It's right here, in the duffel.'' Peggy's fingers froze on the zipper. Her eyes flitted to the electronics store window—and then she exhaled a whoosh of breath. ''Oh, no,'' she whispered, feeling suddenly dizzy.

The window was full of stacked television sets tuned to a true-crime show she'd watched often called *To Catch A Thief*. Right now, her picture—the very same one in Oliver's hand—was displayed on every screen.

His gaze followed hers. ''Great,'' he muttered. ''I can't find you for days and now you're everywhere.''

Instinctively, she clasped her hand over his forearm to steady herself. Surely, he'd believed her story! But maybe not, she decided. It was impossible to tell. Her gaze searched his, but it remained inscrutable. In fact, he looked almost disinterested as he continued studying the televisions.

Image upon image of her face was there for the whole world to see. Another wave of dread washed over her. This all seemed so impossible...so unreal. Her knees buckled, and for a second, she was sure they'd go right out from under her. She wished the sidewalk would open and swallow her up. ''I'm not Susan Jones,'' she whispered hoarsely. ''You have to believe me.''

Could someone really get away with putting her

picture into a criminal database and attaching it to a list of another person's crimes? That was nearly as crazy as seeing herself on *To Catch A Thief.*

"The picture must have been in the FBI computers before today," she managed to murmur. "That's why that man…Kevin Hall…chased me." Fear threatened to overwhelm her. Where could she turn for help? "If Miles did this, can he get away with it? Can he really ruin my life this way?" A soft cry escaped her lips. "What if Mom and Aunt Jill see this? And people at work?"

"There she is!"

Just as the shout sounded from inside the electronics store, Oliver grasped her arm. "C'mon," he said. "There's not much time."

After that, everything happened in a whirlwind. Peggy wrenched to stare over her shoulder at the young Asian man who'd identified her. He was running toward the front door of the store, clearly intending to apprehend her. As Oliver urged her toward Seventh Avenue, a weight lifted from her shoulders. Only belatedly did she realize he'd taken the duffel and slung it over his own shoulder.

"Taxi!" He lifted his arm to hail one.

Following his lead, she waved her arms. "Taxi!"

She was struggling to keep from slipping on the ice as a cab swerved to the curb. Opening the door, Oliver swung the duffel inside then pushed her onto the seat. He followed, hopping inside and flashing his badge at the driver, who turned and glanced over the seat. It was an older cab, with no Plexiglas between the seats.

"Ignore those people chasing us," Oliver said, his voice ringing with authority. "I'm FBI. Here's my badge. It's okay. Go to Seventy-fifth and Madison."

Silently, the driver did as he was told.

"Seventy-fifth and Madison?" Peggy whispered. Thankful for the heat, she thrust her frozen fingers toward the vents to warm them as she turned in the seat to look out the back windshield. The man who'd given chase had stopped in the street. He was pointing at the cab, yelling toward the store where a second man was punching in numbers on a cell phone, probably calling the police.

As her eyes darted to Oliver, Peggy realized she'd wound up wedged against him. All at once, the enclosed car seemed incredibly small. Now she noticed that a Christmas song was playing on the radio, and the feelings brought by the warmth and music threatened to tear down the defensive wall she'd erected around herself. Tears stung her eyes as she watched a car deodorizer shaped like a tiny Christmas tree swing from where it was looped over the rearview mirror.

"Sorry," she murmured, scooting to give Oliver room.

Everything in his eyes said he hadn't minded the contact. His voice was gruff. "No problem."

She was still wondering what was on Seventy-fifth and Madison. For all she knew, he was taking her to FBI headquarters, after all. "Where are we going?"

He glanced toward the cabdriver, and then, as if he feared the man might overhear him, he simply said, "You'll see."

8

FROM SEVENTY-FIFTH and Madison, Oliver had hailed another cab to bring them back downtown in case they'd been followed from the electronics store, and during that ride, since Plexiglas was between the seats, he'd risked sharing what little he knew, starting with the day Anna had crossed the Sex Files with Quick Composite.

"I can't believe you actually did that," Peggy had whispered. "I was watching the *Rise and Shine* show when Kate Olsen suggested it."

Oliver had explained he'd been working with the Most Wanted list when Anna inputted the Sex Files statistics, which was how he'd wound up in possession of Peggy's picture. He'd conceded that Miles could have put the picture into the FBI's database, linking it with Susan Jones's rap sheet, killing two birds with one stone. It forced Peggy into hiding, making it difficult for her to know whom to trust or where to turn for help. Meantime, people were looking for her, not for the real Susan Jones.

"She's a very nondescript woman," Peggy had put in. "Five foot five. One hundred thirty pounds. Brown hair. Blue eyes." She'd listed the woman's statistical information as if she, herself, was an agent, adding credence to her claims of being a crime buff.

Once they were safely inside Anna and Vic's apartment, Oliver had made Peggy slowly repeat the story she'd told him in the street, which she did, reiterating how frightened she'd been to return to her own apartment, and how Kevin Hall had chased her through the subway. Then Oliver had made some phone calls, turned the radio to Christmas music and set about making hot cocoa. Now, as he slowly stirred in milk, he glanced over the gleaming white kitchen island at Peggy, who was seated on a bar stool; she was petting Midnight who, in turn, had curled in her lap. She still hadn't taken off her coat.

But she was definitely Peggy Fox.

Even when Anna had first brought up her picture on the computer screen, Oliver had sworn he recognized her from somewhere; when she'd identified the airline she worked for, it had clicked. He couldn't name a specific time, but he was sure she'd been an attendant on one of the flights he'd taken while touring with his book. With a face like hers, you'd think he'd recall the exact flight, but then, just as Anna kept reminding him, he'd been working a grueling schedule, sometimes fourteen-hour days.

Even if he hadn't recognized Peggy, she was telling the truth about her identity. As soon as they'd come inside, she'd primly placed a New York driver's license on the countertop. Now he winced, trying not to dwell on how insensitive he'd been. Everything in her story seemed to be checking out, which meant she'd really been on the run for weeks, needing his help.

"Nice place," she murmured now, sounding wistful, her eyes trailing around the apartment. He'd left off the overhead light in favor of two small lamps with red-and-green stained-glass shades.

"Small." The one-bedroom had a large combined living room–dining room, and a kitchen was separated by the island.

"But it's got a working fireplace. I didn't know they still existed in walk-up buildings."

"That's why Anna and Vic took this place."

"It's cozy."

And with only the two of them in it, Oliver couldn't help but wonder if it was going to get even cozier. He glanced toward the exposed-brick wall and rough-hewn mantel. Last week, he'd bought some chopped wood from the tree lot near Bleeker Street. "If you'd like, I'll build you a fire. It's a good night for it."

"That would be great," she murmured, her shoulders shaking slightly as if she was suppressing a shudder, her eyes still flitting around the room, as though she couldn't quite believe she'd landed somewhere safe and warm.

He tried not to think of the needy way she'd clung to him in the shower at the Washington Square Hotel. What a fool he'd been! He'd been so hot to make love to her that he hadn't even registered her fear. It was unlike him not to be more aware. But that night, she'd come to him for help and all he could see was a satisfying lay. Now he wanted to make that up to her by offering her the help she'd initially sought. He'd been prepared to haul her in for questioning, but as he'd listened to her on Bleeker Street, her wild story had started to seem plausible, especially when she'd mentioned Miles McLaughlin's white Jaguar. The car, like everything about Miles, was too flashy. Night and day from Oliver's six-year-old Toyota.

Over Peggy's shoulder, Oliver could see the thickening snowfall. Driving in sheets against a steady northerly wind, the flakes sparkled under the streetlamps like fairy dust. Someone inside the nightclub across the street had closed the curtains, so he and Peggy were spared the black-light strobe. "It's quieter than usual tonight." He shook his head. "Some nights, the club across the street really rocks."

"I know," she returned. "I set up camp across the street one night, trying to get a sense of whether to approach you."

"I saw you." He chuckled softly. "I thought you were a computer image come to life."

The color on her china-pale cheeks heightened. "Cameron? America's Sexiest Woman?" She eyed him with disbelief. "How could a…"

"Law enforcement officer believe such a thing?"

She nodded. "Yeah."

"I didn't," he defended. "Not really." He shrugged, looking as close to sheepish as a man like Oliver Vargo could ever get. "But I'd seen the picture. And there didn't seem to be a reasonable explanation for your appearance." He added, "And you are sexy."

She acknowledged the comment with only the

slightest nod, in deference to the fact that they were alone in the apartment. He wasn't surprised. Anything more than that, and he'd circle the island and kiss her. That would only be the beginning.

She said, "I wasn't sure if you knew Miles or not. And after Kevin chased me, I was afraid to approach you."

Oliver didn't blame her for wondering if he was trustworthy. It wasn't every day an average citizen caught a law enforcement agent with a known felon. "Television shows often make it look as if dirty cops are a dime a dozen, but that's not really the case. I've no idea if Kevin knows what Miles is up to." He shook his head, still barely able to believe Peggy's story. Miles was a jerk, yes. Even narcissistic. But had he really crossed the line? Was he involved with a fugitive? Had money Susan Jones taken from a heist really been in his Jaguar? Had he stood aside in an isolated airport parking lot and watched Susan fire a gun shot at Peggy? "Miles and I aren't close," he added.

"Good," she said in an almost whisper.

He was glad to be inside, out of the cold, and he could barely believe how swiftly the relationship between him and Peggy was seeming to shift gears. He was assuming she'd spend the night. Where else could she go? If Miles and Susan Jones were really involved—and if they knew Peggy was aware of the relationship, and knew she'd seen the money—then she really couldn't go to her apartment which, as it turned out, was only a few blocks away. In fact, she shouldn't leave *this* apartment until he could get the evidence necessary to turn Miles in.

He sighed. The idea of Peggy being trapped in Anna's apartment while he got to the bottom of all this didn't bother him in the least. He imagined spending passionate nights on the faux-bearskin rug Anna kept in front of the fireplace. Then he felt guilty. Dammit, the woman had come to him for help. "You'll need to stay here," he murmured. "If you want, I'll take the couch."

She nodded noncommittally, and when she spoke, she shifted the subject; there was another, almost mournful catch in her voice. "There's a Christmas tree here."

He nodded toward a blue spruce that could never pass for real. "Anna, my sister, decorated it for me." For so long, he'd thought of her as Anna's friend; now it was hard to imagine the truth—that the two women had never met. Vaguely, he wondered if they would...if this new interlude with the woman he now knew to be Peggy would lead somewhere as interesting as the places they'd already been together. "She felt sorry for me, since I'm spending Christmas here alone."

"It's only a few days away," she said quietly. Lights had ignited in her eyes, and for a second, he experienced the optical illusion that there were candles dancing inside them. "Cute," she remarked.

He chuckled softly. "Some tree, huh?"

That got a smile out of her. Lifting a hand, she brushed away a lock of hair that had fallen in front of her eye. "Different."

For a moment, they took in the decorated tree, enjoying the red glow from lights that were shaped like chili peppers. A long string of silver beads interspersed with faux heads of garlic served as a garland. No two ornaments were alike. "Midnight likes it," Oliver commented with a smile.

"He's climbing it?" she guessed.

"Yeah. Look," he added as he poured the cocoa into waiting mugs and topped them off with cream he'd whipped earlier in the day. "Everything's going to work out fine."

"Your lips to God's ears."

His mouth curled upward at the familiar saying, since it was one he'd heard his mother use often. "Really," he continued soothingly, placing the mug in front of Peggy. "I'm sorry I..." His mind cast around for the right words. "That I didn't realize you needed help." Not that he was sorry about what had happened between them. Kissing her in the street had only rekindled his desire. He wanted her now more than ever.

When her eyes captured his, they held the same awareness he'd noticed on Bleeker Street when she'd kissed him. He guessed she still wanted him, too. "You believe me then?"

"You're definitely Peggy Fox," he returned easily. "And you do work for the airline." That was one of the places he'd called as soon as they'd come in; the other was Anna's hotel. Peggy had phoned her mother and Aunt Jill in Ohio, but apparently they hadn't seen her picture on TV as she had feared.

"Are you sure it won't hurt to call?" she'd asked him, looking relieved.

He'd shaken his head. "It's doubtful Miles is checking their calls. Even if he is, I secured this line when I moved in. They don't give out my phone records."

"Not even to Miles?"

"No," he'd said. "I'm senior to Miles."

As she'd talked to her relatives, Oliver had admired her ingenuity. In case someone in her mother's neighborhood had recognized her, she'd chuckled softly, saying, "Well, I just wanted to phone. Someone who's the spitting image of me was shown on one of those true-crime shows—I think it was *To Catch A Thief*. Just in case you're alarmed and think I've morphed into a bank robber named Susan Jones—"

She'd laughed then, the sound so light and airy that Oliver would never have believed she'd spent these past weeks in trouble. Listening to her, he'd felt a world of things he hadn't felt in a long time. Admiration for her bravery. Tenderness since she loved her family too much to involve them in something that could be dangerous.

There was an odd sense of familiarity, too, since the life she'd come from in Ohio seemed so much like the one his folks shared in Utah. From what he could catch between the lines, her mother was baking Christmas cookies for a church potluck while Aunt Jill worked on a needlepoint she intended to frame. As he listened to the conversation, he'd found himself deciding that his family would be compatible with Peggy's. He was surprised to find himself thinking along those lines, but he did want to settle down, didn't he? Wasn't that why he'd bought a house? And wasn't Cameron—aka Peggy—more intriguing than any prospect in a long time?

"I'm only away this Christmas," Peggy had assured her relatives before she'd hung up, the love she felt obvious from her tone. "During the holiday travel rush they always need extra flight attendants, Mom," she'd said, "so I've been lucky this is the only year they've asked me to work."

Now she said, "If you help figure out what's going on, Oliver, maybe all this will get straightened out and I can go home."

The mournful look on her face was definitely hard to take, and more than anything, it convinced him she wasn't capable of wrongdoing. "I can tell you miss your mother and aunt." After a pause, he added, "I miss my folks, too."

"Do you have a good time in Utah?"

He nodded. "The consummate Christmas. Turkey and trimmings. Presents and long walks in the woods. Anna and I make snowmen in the front yard as if we're still kids."

"You grew up there, right?"

He shook his head. "No. Couldn't you tell by my accent? We grew up here. In Manhattan. That's why Anna stayed. I didn't stray far, only to the Virginia– D.C. area."

She squinted. "Why did your parents go all the way to Utah?"

"They were ready for a big change. They had fantasies about trying a sort of life they'd never lived.

Dad was able to take early retirement. He was a schoolteacher. Mom's a nurse, so she was able to start work again as soon as they moved.''

For a moment, Miles McLaughlin and Susan Jones seemed a million miles away from Peggy's mind. "So, Utah's not really home turf for you?"

He shook his head again. "Nope. I think that's why Anna and I love it so much. It's a novelty. Wide skies. Lots of stars. Peace and quiet."

"Would you live there?"

He was surprised that his response wasn't immediate, that something so simple as answering her question could feel like a risk. For all he knew, it was her life dream to live in Utah, and he felt like pleasing her more than he wanted to admit. He stuck to the truth. "No. I'm a city boy. Utah's a nice place, but…"

"Sounds perfect for a visit."

"You?"

She narrowed her eyes thoughtfully. "Me?"

"Yeah. Would you live someplace else?"

She shrugged. "I don't know. New York's been exciting, but I do miss Ohio. I like having more space. Room to move around. Maybe I'll even get some sort of desk job eventually."

His eyebrows raised. "You're not happy?"

Tilting her head and considering, she said, "Things are different now with the airlines. Honestly, since September eleventh, I'm afraid to fly sometimes. I feel bad about that." She paused. "And what's happening to me now definitely makes the city seem even more dangerous."

"You're not obligated to be one of the brave people."

"But if you give in," she said, "terrorists win, right?" And evil people like Miles McLaughlin.

"Not if you have other aspirations, anyway."

"I do, actually. A safe, quiet home somewhere. Sometimes, I miss the simple life my mom and Aunt Jill share." Something dark and unreadable crossed her features. "Right now, to tell you the truth, I just want to stay alive. I've felt that my job was dangerous, but after being shot at…"

His heart wrenched. "You've been running scared, haven't you? I'm sorry. We just got to talking about Christmas, and for a minute, I forgot what you've been through."

"No," she said quickly. "Please don't apologize. This has all been so crazy. I can't believe I just saw my own picture on *To Catch A Thief*. It seems so impossible. Right now, talking about Christmas makes me feel better. I just wish this one was different."

He thought of the Christmas tree he usually cut with his dad. "Me, too. This one definitely isn't the same. But you're going to be fine. I can promise that."

"You can?"

His eyes caught hers, and he stared deeply into the soft brown irises. "I'll protect you. Keep you safe until we can figure this out."

"Thanks."

His mouth suddenly quirked. "It may not be our

usual Christmas. However, you have to admit, this one's shaping up to be interesting."

"Isn't it, though?" As if the thought was too over-whelmingly depressing for her to bear, Peggy lifted the mug to her lips, blew across the top and took a sip. Her eyes widened in surprise at the taste. "This is great." Glancing toward the nutmeg and cinnamon he'd left on the counter, she added, "Really. This is the best cocoa I've ever tasted, Oliver."

"The trick is adding brown sugar." Circling the island, he came to stand next to her, sidling closer than was necessary. From the new spot, he could catch her female scent; it wafted to him, smelling as enticing as the spices he'd put in their drinks. "My mom makes it this way."

She took another sip, and his heart suddenly stilled when he noted the cream mustache left behind. Fighting the urge to lean and kiss it off, he settled for gliding a hand over the back of one of hers.

Her eyes swept to his. "You really do believe me, don't you, Oliver?"

Not really. He believed the gist of what she'd said, but Oliver also suspected she'd omitted details. Call it his sixth sense. He'd spent years interviewing better liars than she, and something about her story didn't ring entirely true. She'd left out some tidbit; there was something she didn't want him to know.

On the other hand, he had enough self-awareness to know that he was suspicious by both trade and nature. So, he could be wrong. "Of course I believe you. Everything you've told me checks out." If some-thing had been omitted, it was only a matter of time until he discovered it. That was the thing about truth—like cream, it always surfaced.

"How could my picture have wound up on TV?" she suddenly mused again, the words touched with enough barely suppressed panic that Midnight raised his head and scrutinized her with yellow eyes. "Sorry," she murmured, lifting her hand from beneath Oliver's so she could slowly stroke Midnight's head.

Oliver watched as if mesmerized while those long slender fingers twirled circles around the cat's ears, then scratched between them. Satisfied, Midnight purred loudly, the sound coming over a reggae version of "Santa Claus is Coming to Town."

"Usually only killers rate a spot on *To Catch A Thief*," Oliver finally said. "But if what you're saying is true, it is possible that Miles used his position and power to put your picture on the show. And he's definitely got the know-how to attach your picture to his girlfriend's rap sheet—if she's his girlfriend."

"You don't believe—"

"It's possible there's some government sting I don't know about, and Miles is only pretending to date her. Right now, Susan Jones is on the run with three million from a heist—"

"I know it's not a sting," Peggy protested. "He's involved with her—and covering for her."

Oliver grunted noncommittally. He wasn't the type to make assessments without evidence. "I don't know. But you're probably right. If you really saw him with Susan Jones—"

"I did!"

"All right," he murmured. "I believe you. Then that explains why he used your picture during a recent meeting where he was touting his new Quick Composite software." He filled Peggy in on the meeting.

"I bet he's planning to skip town with her."

Skip town. It was the kind of phrase writers used in crime fiction, and hearing it, as well as the hitch in her voice, he was once more convinced that she'd been telling the truth about being a crime buff. Oliver had met many. At every cocktail party he'd ever attended, at least one person had wanted to share an opinion with him about the latest national crime story. Usually, the people secretly fancied themselves as an undiscovered Sherlock Holmes or Miss Marples.

Fortunately, as near as Oliver could tell, the attempt on Peggy's life had cured her of any such romantic notions. At least he hoped so. Nevertheless, she had a point. "It's risky. But it's possible," he finally said. "He has the power to do it. And an agent's salary will never keep him in the high style that Susan Jones can. Plus, you said you saw the money."

"I'm sure I did. But could he really erase Susan Jones from the FBI files?" Peggy asked. "And scan my picture onto her rap sheet instead? It seems…"

"Crazy. Yeah, it does. But you were nearly killed, and it sent you underground, into hiding. You saw the two of them together, and you were afraid to go to the police."

"Since he was in law enforcement, I was confused," she admitted.

Chewing his lower lip, Oliver thought of Miles's new "paperless" FBI, then gave Peggy the rundown on it. "The drive to destroy paper documents has largely been Miles's baby," he finished. "It really might be difficult to find her picture right now. And without easy-to-access backup evidence, it's feasible that a crooked agent with the right codes and passwords could pull this off." Insane, Oliver thought, but feasible. He compressed his lips. What better word was there to describe criminals but insane?

"I'll have to find out more tomorrow," he added. "Maybe I can get a phone log and trace some of his incoming calls. Maybe we can track Susan Jones that way. I'll see if the two have any previous contact. Maybe Miles arrested her in the past. The office is swept for bugs once a week, and the sweepers were there this morning, so I can bug Miles's office without getting caught. I'll double-check to see if there's some kind of sting operation, too—in case there's another explanation—"

"Other than?"

"The things we're supposing."

"I think we're right."

"Me, too." He sighed. "Call it instinct."

He was rewarded with a touch. Lifting her hand from Midnight's head, she slid those slender fingers over the back of his hand and let them rest there. It was just shy of an invitation, so he treated it as such, edging closer. Heat from her side traveled to his.

She blew out a sigh. "I can't believe you're really going to help me. I'm so relieved."

Right now, staring into her eyes, there was very little he wouldn't do for her. Shaking his head, he cursed softly under his breath. "Given Miles's access to other database systems, the man could do a lot of damage.'' Oliver frowned. ''You're positive the woman was Susan Jones?''

Her voice caught with the bafflement of the honest and innocent when confronted with somebody who chose the wrong side of the law. ''Yes. And like I said, she tried to shoot me...'' Peggy paused. ''...in the parking lot.''

It was hard to stomach the idea. Had an agent really watched as a known felon attempted to kill an innocent woman? Oliver wondered once more. ''What happened then?''

''I ran.'' Pausing, she swallowed hard. ''I...uh, ducked down behind some other parked cars. Crouched down and ran along the bumpers...''

''I'm sorry that happened to you,'' he whispered.

''It's not your fault.''

He shook his head, considering Miles's personality type. ''I've worked closely with him,'' he murmured. ''He's boastful and egotistical. Flashy. His wardrobe and the car you mentioned aren't really suitable for an FBI agent. I've always thought he's probably a narcissistic personality.''

She squinted curiously as she took another sip of cocoa. ''Meaning?''

He suddenly smiled. Right now, seeing the curiosity in her gaze, he was reminded of Anna, who was always asking him to clarify himself in what she called ''real-people speak.'' Except this wasn't Anna, of course. This was a woman he'd enjoyed in bed. A woman he wanted again. A brave woman who was in danger, who'd chosen not to involve her family members at all in order to protect them. Unexpected anger flared inside him before he tamped it down, and for that instant, he felt he'd kill anybody who laid a hand on Peggy Fox.

"Narcissistic personalities can become grandiose," he continued. "Convinced of their own invincibility. The development of such a personality type is usually in reaction to having a troubled childhood. People get hurt, have a damaged sense of self—"

"That's sad, Oliver."

"It is. And often not dangerous. But sometimes, when hurt people react and become egotistical enough, they can hurt others. If he was grandiose enough, Miles could trot Susan Jones into FBI headquarters and believe he could get away with it. Sometimes, people do exactly what Miles might have done—take wild risks, hoping to get caught."

"A cry for help?"

"Exactly."

She was watching him closely. "You really are a criminal profiler, huh?"

"Absolutely."

"It just seems so strange," she went on, grappling with what he'd said. "I mean, Miles will definitely get caught, right? I'm obviously not Susan Jones. I've been carrying my identification cards. And what about all the people who know me? My mother? Or Aunt Jill? My grade-school teachers still remember me." She groaned. "And like I said, what if people at the airline saw me on TV?"

"Don't worry. It'll work out. We just need a few days."

She sighed again. "Well…no one called Mom yet." Setting down her mug, she swiveled on the bar stool to face him. The movement brought her knees to his, just enough that the caps brushed. At the relatively innocent contact, both Oliver and Peggy inhaled sharply, simultaneously drawing audible breaths. She exhaled first, saying, "There's a whole world of people who can verify I'm not Susan Jones or a fugitive from justice."

Hating to be the grim bearer of bad tidings, Oliver pointed out, "As long as no hotshot agent shoots first and asks questions later. Susan Jones is a career criminal. Guys in my business will get brownie points for taking her down."

He could see her throat working as she swallowed. "Do you think Kevin Hall knew the truth about Miles and Susan?"

Oliver considered. "I don't know. Probably not. He looks up to Miles, but Kevin's a follower, not a leader."

"That's his M.O., huh?"

He smiled at her use of law enforcement lingo. "His modus operandi. Yep."

She edged forward on the stool as if perched to run, a move that sent Midnight hopping to the counter. Stretching, the black cat arched his back and yawned before pivoting and leaping to the floor. "At this point," she said, watching Midnight head for the tree, where he rolled luxuriously beneath it on a white, glitter-sparkled tree skirt. "No one will be able to pinpoint who tampered with those computer files, right? No one will be able to prove beyond a doubt who attached my picture to Susan Jones's rap sheet. I mean, there's probably no record pointing to Miles McLaughlin.''

Leaning closer, Oliver couldn't help but lift a hand and brush back that errant lock of hair that kept falling in front of her eye. He found himself rubbing the strands between his thumb and forefinger, the sensation of silk seeming to linger even after he pushed the hair aside.

"I'm not sure," he admitted. "You'll just have to be patient. After we snoop a little, it's possible that a computer expert can find out something more. Maybe even identify the specific computer from which the changes to the database were made." He shrugged. Crimes were solved in hour-long episodes only on TV. "Honestly," he added. "It'll take some time. I wish I was better with computers. Anna's the whiz, not me.''

"Computers aren't my strong point, either," she confessed.

Oliver sent her another smile of encouragement. Most probably, Miles was a dirty agent with a criminal lover—and about to leave town with money from her bank heist. "Despite our computer deficits," he found himself murmuring, his voice becoming husky, "there are things we can do."

She looked so hopeful that he almost leaned and kissed her. He wasn't sure why he refrained. Maybe to prolong the agony—and make their lovemaking that much sweeter. "Tomorrow, I'll check for any link between Susan Jones and Miles," he said again. "Maybe he arrested or questioned her before, like you said," she remarked approvingly. "Good thinking."

"Thanks." He glanced toward her empty mug. "Feel better after the cocoa?"

She nodded. "Yeah. Maybe we could order some take-out, too." Before he could respond, she apologized again, adding, "I should have gone to the police, but I really didn't know what to do. And since I'd read your books and saw you on TV…"

He realized he was only inches away from her. It couldn't be helped. The woman drew him like a magnet. He'd tilted his head and brought it lower as if he meant to kiss her. Hell, maybe he did. When he spoke, his voice came out sounding throaty. "I'm glad you wanted my help, Peggy."

"I was so scared. You…" She took a deep breath, those dark eyes now searching his face in a way that made him want to haul her into his arms. "You seemed like the best."

Another slow smile spread over his features. "I *am* the best."

She chuckled softly at that, even though the worry hadn't quite left her eyes. "Modest, too."

It wasn't the first time she'd said it. "You know better than that." For a moment, he let the words linger, let her remember the bold way he'd stepped into the shower with her, aroused and naked.

"Why don't you take off your coat?" he suggested then, the downward drift of his eyes making clear he'd like to see her *sans* the rest of her outfit, too. "You're about Anna's size, and she's got a whole closetful of clothes that might be more comfortable."

Once more, her cheeks grew flushed and her eyes brightened in a way that made him hope she wasn't really going to make him sleep on the couch. She offered a soft, embarrassed chuckle. "I usually don't wear things like this. As I said, I asked Kiki to bring the clothes…"

He bit back a shudder as he recalled the lingerie in the duffel. In particular, his mind reviewed a crimson garter belt and a sheer bodysuit. "If you ask me," he couldn't help but say, feeling a pang of pleasure as his groin flexed, "Kiki's got great taste. I'd like to see you wearing jeans and a sweatshirt, but…"

"But you're a guy, right?"

"Right."

Something dry hit the back of his throat, and suddenly he could scarcely swallow. "Look," he managed to say, shifting his weight and wishing he wasn't getting so obviously aroused. "I know you came to me for help. And I'm going to help you, Peggy…" *But I want you.* An erection was pressuring his fly, demanding to be satisfied—and he hadn't even touched the woman yet. If he'd ever get to again. Lightly, he licked his lips, waiting for her to say something.

Questions were in her eyes. "What are we, uh…"

"Going to do over the next few days?" He shrugged, not sure exactly what part of their relationship she wanted to clarify. He'd kissed her in the street tonight, yes. But then, he'd been angry. Now things were different, and they were inside his sister's apartment, and he really would sleep on the sofa, if that's what she wanted. "I need a couple days to find out what I can," he finally said. "You need to stay here. Since your apartment's so close, you shouldn't go out at all. Not even to the deli for milk. Just in case Susan Jones has your address and is looking for you.''

She shook her head. ''I hope my roommates aren't in any danger.''

''Very doubtful. She's after you. And, honestly, I don't really understand why she took that shot at you. She's a thief, not a killer. She has absolutely no history that would indicate she's inclined toward violence. Speaking as a profiler, it just doesn't make sense. Attempted murder isn't her M.O.''

''But I saw the money.''

''True. Maybe that made you a different kind of threat. Still…'' Pausing, he frowned as if the issue would require further thought. ''Anyway, you're safe here.''

There was a long pause.

''Oliver,'' she suddenly said, ''I really don't know if this is a good idea. I mean, I don't think you and I should…uh…''

Usually, he'd simply do the gentlemanly thing and accept whatever she wanted. It was a lady's job to call the limits. But with her, things were different. ''What?'' he said, refusing to skirt the issue. ''Co-habitate?''

She nodded.

''Well, we are.'' He brought his mouth to hover above hers.

Her breath was spiced with brown sugar he could almost taste. ''Oliver,'' she said in warning.

He was sorry to hear the protest. She wanted safety, after all, right? Loving? Comfort? Whatever her reason for not wanting this, the tantalizing kiss he delivered was calculated to make her forget it. His mouth settled firmly but without demand. Gently, he used his lips to part hers, only slightly at first before opening farther so she could take his tongue.

Despite her verbal protest, she returned the kiss, matching the movements of his mouth, her lips fitting perfectly to his, latching and holding on. His hips arched, seeking her, hers pushed back, and he knew she was getting damp for him. Just like he was getting harder for her.

Soon, he'd press his fingers inside the tunnel of her slick wet heat. Or at least he hoped so. It had been weeks since their encounter in the hotel, but not ten minutes had passed without him remembering how it felt to be inside her. Thrusting his tongue, he deepened the kiss as his hands circled her waist, then dexterously untied the belt to her raincoat. "I missed you," he whispered, nuzzling his whisker-roughened jaw against her softer, creamier, decidedly feminine cheek.

"If you really want me to sleep on the couch, I will," he murmured. "But ever since we had sex, I've been thinking about us being together again."

Dragging his mouth across hers, he pushed aside the parted fabric of her coat, then pressed flattened palms to her rounded belly, slipping them around her waist. When he felt her skin quiver beneath his fingertips, passion flooded him, and the push of his tongue turned darker, communicating intention. He was touching the sort of confection most men only dreamed of a women wearing, and when he glanced down, he saw that the raw silk dress was brown, the color of eyes that were glazing with need.

"I called in sick so I could search the city for you," he muttered, his lips tracing hers as he spoke. "I looked everywhere. I had to find you."

Her voice caught as she leaned back her head, offering her neck for a trail of languorous kisses. "To arrest me."

"Maybe," he returned, his voice so low it was barely audible. "But since then, I've thought of many other things we can do."

"Ah. So, you're keeping me here as a hostage?"

"Sounds good to me."

Arms she'd wreathed around his neck tightened. A second later, he felt her hands drag upward. Splayed fingers raked into his hair, her nails kneading his scalp. Glancing down, he saw that her face was red from the burn of his whiskers, and that her mouth was ever redder.

He took it again—and again—capturing her lips from one angle, then another, each renewed onslaught becoming more fierce as he wedged a knee between her legs. When she didn't open immediately, he urged with his thigh, then he took a step closer, sending that thigh higher between her parting legs...then higher...until suddenly she was riding him, grinding against him for her pleasure. "Tell me if you really want me to stop," he whispered.

"I don't," she whispered back.

"You don't want me to sleep on the couch?"

Drawing in an audible breath, she said, "No."

That's when he knew they'd make love here. Like this. The bed could come later. He wanted that, too.

He could almost feel the rocking waves of the water, how they'd gently lift her hips, bringing her to him. The hem of the dress had risen, and his mouth had turned greedy. She was clinging more tightly as their tongues met, melded and moved together in perfect concert. As he ground his thigh against her, the movement both rough and gentle, bespeaking a desire to love and a desire to take, he felt her start to shake.

"I want you," he repeated, the words lost when he sucked a breath of need through his teeth. Reaching, he plucked her breasts, grasping the nipples, until she gasped. Leaning back a fraction, just enough to enjoy the ecstasy on her face, he rolled the peaks between his fingertips, watching them bead against the silk, murmuring, "Yes," when a sob was wrenched from her throat.

Feeling a need to torture, just as she'd tortured him for so many weeks, he pinched ever so lightly, then pulled her closer, tugging the aroused tips now—all the while watching her go wild from the sensations. As she arched, thrusting her aching breasts toward his hands, frustration coursed through him. As much as he wanted this to last, his body was demanding more. And yet when her hands reached to touch him intimately, he edged away. Yes, he wanted this to last just another moment longer…

"I never thought I'd see you again," he murmured, taking her mouth again.

"Me, neither." She sighed. "I was going to leave New York. I didn't know what to do…"

"This," he murmured. "This is what you should do. You should be here with me."

His mouth caught her sob of longing, and he

dropped both hands to her thighs, pushing up the silk so he could feel the sweet groove where her legs met her torso. His thumbs fell into the hollows, tracing and bracketing her mound, exerting more pressure until she arched from the bar stool, seeking his touch, leaving no doubt that she was as ready as he. "After I saw the picture of you, I started having fantasies about you," he whispered. "Wild, hot, sexy fantasies."

"Me, too."

He squinted in disbelief. "When?"

"After I saw your picture in your book," she returned, her voice catching. "And when I saw you on TV."

Hooking a finger into the leg bands of the string she wore for panties, he pulled them down her legs. And then he simply dropped to his knees.

She gasped at the swift, unexpected movement, then writhed when his hands slid around her backside, hauling her to him. He buried his face then, pressing deeply against her, using his whiskered cheeks to roughen her open thighs. His mind blanked with need as his tongue found her center.

Slowly and deeply, he stroked her intimately with the wet spear of his tongue, opening her completely. Everything was happening so fast. Too fast, he thought vaguely. One moment, they'd been drinking cocoa, and he'd said he was going to sleep on the couch. The next, he was going down on her in the kitchen and loving every second. Using a restraint he couldn't believe he had, he circled her bud with his tongue until she was drenched. As the love knot tightened, her building cries shot through him, ripping through his veins. She wrenched, but there was no-where for her to go, except more deeply against his mouth. Convulsing, she grasped his hair with her hands.

A moment later, he rose to his feet, dragging down his zipper. Pushing down his briefs, he simply entered her with a driving upward thrust. The feeling of flesh against flesh was too much to bear. "I didn't…didn't think I'd find you," he muttered raggedly, the broken words breaking over her ear.

"I'm here," she gasped, her mouth on his shoulder now, the kiss she planted there sweet and wet. Her teeth followed, nipping his skin, just hard enough to shoot darts of pleasure into his bloodstream as her hips met his.

And then he was gone.

Everything turned dark. There was only her—slick and tight, with a scent like honey. As she crested again, the tunnel of her body pulsing, suckling at his shaft, he threw his head back. He waited until the very last possible second before he pulled away, coming outside her body, since he hadn't used a condom.

"I missed you," he uttered once more.

This time, Peggy laughed, and he was glad to hear the fear gone from her voice, if only for a moment. She was still panting when she said, "You don't really need to mention that, Oliver."

"Why not?"

He felt her smile against his skin. "Because I can tell."

9

"I ASKED YOU not to go out." A twinge of scarcely concealed anger was in Oliver's voice as he came inside the next evening, his eyes trailing over the open grocery bag on the kitchen countertop, and the items Peggy had used to cook dinner.

"Sorry," Peggy murmured, guilt rushing in on her since he'd looked so happy when he'd first stepped across the threshold. Now his eyes were narrowing suspiciously, taking in the open cans of tuna fish, box of noodles and open bag of potato chips. She watched as he scanned the apartment as if he half expected to find her having tea with Susan Jones, then he locked the door. Drawing a heavy black box from under his arm, he headed for the living room without saying anything further and began fiddling with the phone extension.

She was half-relieved at the tension. And he was right, of course. She shouldn't have gone out. But she'd really wanted to make him a tuna casserole from Aunt Jill's recipe. Now the only upside to his mood, she supposed, was that if they were fighting, maybe they wouldn't wind up in bed again. The rational part of her wanted to sleep on the couch tonight—or for him to—but the lust-driven vixen Oliver had aroused wanted to walk across the living room, grab him by the collar and haul his mouth to hers. It had been for good reason that she'd sworn off men. Taking a deep breath, Peggy surveyed the black box and called, "What are you doing?"

"I bugged Miles's phone," he said gruffly, speaking over his shoulder as he placed some headphones on an end table.

Glad he'd given up the previous topic, Peggy continued sprinkling cracker crumbs over the top of the casserole, barely noticing when he stood, unbuttoned his overcoat and strode toward the kitchen. Sensing his temper, Midnight hopped from a bar stool to the floor and fled for the bedroom.

"Now," he said, stopping behind her as she stretched to put the casserole into the microwave. "Why'd you go out?"

So much for hoping he'd forgotten the topic. Glancing quickly over her shoulder, she spun the dial on the timer and said, "I'm really sorry, Oliver. I know I shouldn't have—"

He muttered something incoherent, dragging a hand through his hair and dislodging snowflakes that had been left there by the winter evening; as they melted into the dark strands, the dim light cast by the lamps made them glisten. He looked thoroughly exasperated. "What were you thinking, Peggy?"

"I wasn't. I just—"

"As scared as you were," he interrupted, "I never thought you'd leave the apartment."

Last night, sleeping in his arms had made her feel safe—maybe too safe. "It was only for a minute."

As Peggy finished dusting crumbs from her palms, his large warm hands settled on her shoulders, and just as she shut the microwave door, he turned her around to face him.

"A minute could have gotten you killed."

"Like I said, I wasn't gone long. I really wanted to make us a casserole. I just went to the Sloan's in Sheridan Square, and..."

Her voice trailed off. How could she explain that this afternoon, when she'd glanced out at the pristine blanket of freshly fallen snow, the world had looked so friendly and benign that she'd been sure a quick trip to the grocery store would be safe? No doubt her sense of well-being had everything to do with the naughty way he'd loved her last night and the hours they'd lain awake afterward, whispering nothings. Now she flushed guiltily. "Honestly, I can't really explain it, Oliver, but my gut told me it was fine to leave. I didn't feel like I was in any danger."

"Your gut," he muttered softly, the words that came from under his breath barely audible. "I see. You're relying on your gut now. Your well-honed instincts. Your vast repertoire of knowledge about how criminals behave."

"Don't get nasty."

"I'm concerned," he corrected.

"I wore a hat, scarf and coat," she defended. "No one could see my face." The way she'd been dressed, her own mother and Aunt Jill wouldn't have recognized her.

"A hat. Now, there's a disguise," he said dryly.

"And coat. And scarf. You're not giving these items the credit they deserve."

Since they were arguing, it was the wrong time to notice how handsome he looked in the dark-chocolate suit, but the man could have just stepped from the cover of *GQ*. Definitely, this wasn't one of the more professorial corduroy outfits he usually wore on TV.

"Nice threads," she couldn't help but remark, hoping to change the subject.

"Thanks," he returned.

"Special occasion?"

"Is this a real question?"

"Sure."

"No other clean clothes," he explained.

She should have guessed. Despite the circumstances, she bit back a flicker of a smile, deciding that Oliver Vargo simply radiated wholesome male energy. He had an orderly mind, but she'd found his clothes wadded in the bottom of a closet, and the refrigerator's offerings consisted of nearly empty take-out cartons. Seeing how much he needed a woman, she'd set about making herself useful. "I washed the clothes," she said.

"In the machine in the basement?"

"Where else?"

"Maybe the Chinese laundry next door."

"I only went to the grocery store," she assured.

"Really?"

"Would I lie?"

"Yes."

There was a long pause. She fought back a flush, thinking of the information she'd withheld, that she'd actually agreed to marry a criminal like Miles. At least she hadn't slept with him, she thought now. He'd pressured her, but she'd always held back. It was as if, deep down, her instincts really had been working for her. Still, she'd believed he loved her, and that the ring he'd given her was real. "I wouldn't really lie," she finally said. "Only little white lies."

He considered, then said, "No lies are little."

For a minute, they simply surveyed each other.

Guiltily, Peggy considered telling him the whole truth, once more, but she really didn't want to explain the deficits in her love life to this accomplished, sexy man. She pushed aside the thoughts, concentrating instead on denying the sparks passing between her and Oliver. It was useless. Her traitorous body refused to recognize that they were generated by anger, not desire.

Maybe she didn't even care. Her nerves were zinging. Her spirit was singing. Butterflies had invaded her belly. While heat coursed through her, feeling like heaven, she noted how the chocolate color of the suit changed his eyes, making them look unfathomably dark. Even with his coat still on, and with just a very quick downward cast of her eyes, Peggy could admire the fit of Oliver's low-slung trousers. A silver-and-lemon striped tie hung against a tailored cream shirt, the pointed finger of it tracing the waistband; circled by a simple black belt, the pants settled right beneath his waist, almost on his hips.

She fought it—determined to distance herself from him now that she'd had the day to think about their relationship—but her eyes lingered in the proximity

of his zipper, anyway. Every inch of fabric contrib-
uted to the overall impression that his body was re-
markably powerful, which Peggy knew it was from
experience. The pants weren't tight, of course, but
there was no mistaking the masculine bulge beneath
the fly.

She blew out a shaky breath. What was she going
to do? Last night had been every bit as satisfying as
their time in the hotel, but she wasn't ready to be
involved again. Suddenly conscious of how she'd
braced herself against the counter, she shifted her
weight from one foot to the other, trying to move
away, but he only stepped closer, trapping her between the counter and his body. At the contact, her
mouth went dry, and she found herself swallowing
around what felt like a lump of sawdust. When her
gaze raised to his, he was staring at her as if he'd
never seen her before, much less shared a bed. Or a
bar stool, she mentally amended. Not to mention a
shower.

"I wanted to make you dinner," she ventured
again, finding her voice, but not feeling surprised
when her words came out sounding raspy. "Last
night, you said you liked tuna casseroles." And Miles
Davis CDs. And reading in bed. And the color blue.

"I do."

"And since I know Aunt Jill's recipe by heart, and
there's no food in the apartment…" Her voice trailed
off. "I was starving."

He leaned inward a fraction, just enough that his
body began pressuring hers, sending jolts of pleasure

through her entire system. "As if I was personally trying to starve you to death."

Breathless, she tried to ignore the growing pressure of the body against hers, but it made her heart miss a beat, then another. All at once, the backs of her knees felt flimsy. From her thighs down, everything was turning to water. "I thought you might be hungry, too—"

"You could have ordered take-out—" Swaying, she firmly planted her hip against the counter, but that didn't stop her mind from flooding with memories of how commanding that mouth could feel on top of hers. His body could feel pretty commanding on top of hers, too. Seemingly oblivious of her reactions to him, he continued. "There are plenty of restaurants in the neighborhood, Peggy. Or you could have waited for me to come home and let me shop."

Home. Shop.

The words were even more disturbing than watching Oliver's sensual mouth. Not because they conjured bodily sensations of his kisses, but because they sounded so incredibly domestic. Somehow, that was unsettling. So was the slow drag of his eyes down her outfit. The look was so assessing that she felt vaguely self-conscious, although the green, long-sleeved T-shirt dress of Anna's was far less revealing than anything else Oliver had ever seen her wear.

Of course, beneath the dress, she was wearing panties Kiki had brought in the duffel. And they were crotchless. As she thought of them, Peggy tried to fight the warmth rising on her cheeks. She simply wouldn't have felt comfortable donning Anna's underwear, and while she didn't really see any point to crotchless panties, Peggy didn't feel right not wearing any panties at all. She'd treated the issue like just one more of life's tough little dilemmas—and she'd worn the panties.

Besides, she'd figured the rest of her clothes would be out of the dryer before Oliver came in from work, not that wearing a thong was much better. He was still staring at her, a mouth she knew could kiss like the devil curled in mild displeasure. "I really am sorry," she apologized.

All he said now was, "Hmm."

She'd have liked nothing more than to avoid this tension. All day she'd been alone. And for the first time in a long time, she'd had time to think. Yes, she shivered every time she thought of how Oliver had loved her last night. And yes, she'd spent part of the day enjoying the memories of snuggling on top of him. Even now, she could recall the strength in his forearms as they wrapped around her back, hugging her tightly and making her feel safe and warm.

But she wasn't interested in men.

She couldn't afford to be. After what had happened with Miles McLaughlin, she wanted time away from relationships. A long time. Maybe forever. Obviously, she needed to become much more aware about her choices. And why not? She was well employed and didn't need a man to take care of her. It was worth it to take time out. Someday, she wanted to marry and have a great family…if she lived.

When an image of Susan Jones flashed into her mind, she shuddered. At least she'd finally turned to

Oliver for help. Soon enough, he'd help straighten out this mess. And once she had time to really mull over her past relationships and correct her mistakes, someone special would come along. That would be the best time to get to know Oliver. When she was sure she understood her mistakes, she'd be ready for that special someone. She wanted to be equal partners—and parents.

Her mom and Aunt Jill had often joked that since love hadn't worked for them, and since the third time was the charm, Peggy's romantic life was bound to turn out perfect in the end. Peggy wasn't nearly as optimistic. What she saw was that she came from a line of women who all had blind spots when it came to bad men. Sometimes, she'd even considered that the Foxes might carry some special gene for it.

Since she knew she couldn't afford to make any more mistakes, she couldn't entirely keep the defensiveness from her tone when she spoke again. "You know, Oliver," she suddenly said, "it's not as if we're keeping house."

He stared at her in disbelief. "To the contrary—" A huge strong hand left her shoulder and settled on her waist, the warmth of it seeping through the jersey fabric of her dress. "For the next few days, we are, Peggy."

"Only because it's necessary."

He looked at her pointedly. "Exactly. For your safety."

"C'mon," she coaxed, edging to the side and wishing he'd give her some room. With him this close, it was difficult to think. The pressure of his body was clouding her thoughts and turning her insides to mush. "Just let it go, Oliver," she added. "I'm fine. Nothing happened to me at the store."

But he was right. Something could have. "I felt edgy," she forced herself to continue, her eyebrow raising with significance, just in case he wanted to take the hint and back away a step. "Cooped up." Much as she felt now. With him standing in front of her, she was dangerously tempted to let him fold her inside his arms. "What did you find out at work, anyway?" she asked, shifting the topic. "Anything?"

As if he couldn't quite help himself, he lifted a finger and stroked it down her cheek. Seeing the concern still in his eyes, guilt flooded her once more. "I really don't like that you went outside," he said simply.

"It won't happen again."

"Promise?"

"Promise," she vowed. Staring into dark eyes that were smoldering with warring emotions, she could have felt a hundred different things, but all she registered was awareness—of the night's silence, of the heavy snowfall visible through the windows and of the warm runny feeling in her belly.

"What?" he murmured, coming closer, his hips locking with hers. "Did you feel like I was trying to tell you what to do? Like I wanted to control you?"

She squinted. "By asking me to stay inside?"

He nodded. "Yeah."

Maybe. But now he was really unnerving her. Why couldn't he just let the issue go? No doubt she was just being paranoid—or driven by guilt—but she half suspected Oliver knew she hadn't told him the whole truth about Miles. Yes, given the penetrating gaze fixed on her, it was as if Oliver wouldn't be satisfied until she broke down and told him about her engagement, an idea far too humiliating to even contemplate. Had she really been foolish enough to take a ring from a crooked FBI agent? One who was sleeping with a felon? The man hadn't exactly kept Susan Jones from shooting at Peggy, either.

Suppressing another shudder, she could still see herself at the Rainbow Room with Miles, leaning forward in a way she knew would show off her cleavage as she tossed back the flute of champagne; she'd finished by catching the gold ring between her teeth, so the diamond—or what she'd thought was a diamond—flashed between her lips. But that sparkling gem hadn't even been made of good glass.

Her heart constricted painfully as she thought of how Miles had taken it from between her lips and slipped it onto her finger. How could a man be so cruel? She tried not to dwell on the power he must have felt, knowing that the diamond wasn't real and that he was sleeping with another woman, a fugitive.

She realized Oliver was watching her carefully. "You think I feel controlled by you?" she managed to say, trying and failing to tamp down the hurt and anger that had just arisen. After all, this wasn't Oliver's fault.

"I don't know. That's why I'm asking."

"Why don't you tell me," she said. "You're the profiler."

"Why are you pushing me away?"

"I'm not sure I like being psychoanalyzed."

"That's not what I'm doing."

"Hmm. I think you're profiling me," she returned, keeping the tone light, "and while you're busy doing that, maybe I should go get the rest of my clothes out of the dryer." Standing this close to Oliver, she would definitely feel better in something other than crotchless panties, which also happened to be red.

"You're already dressed." His voice lowered a notch. "And I like it." After a pause, he added, "Very much. You look good in green."

The gaze that dropped down the jersey fabric was hot enough that it could have been an iron. As it swept past her breasts, the tips tightened visibly, beading, and his eyes glinted with awareness. Something scalding seemed to flush through her veins, and the surface of her skin turned prickly. The next thing she knew, she was thinking of the panties again. Inhaling another quavering breath, she tried to ignore that she was getting damp for him, and that absolutely no fabric was there to capture the moisture.

"Thank you," she said, her voice hitching with nervousness or anticipation, she wasn't sure which. "I'm glad you like the dress, I really am. Um, look, Oliver…" She was determined to recover the situation, but when she inadvertently cast a glance toward the stool where he'd begun making love to her the previous night, another wave of awareness washed over her. "Dinner will be ready in a few minutes," she continued, feeling strangely valiant for talking at all, given the fact that the man's nearness was still making her knees feel like rubber. "If you'd rather talk than let me get the clothes out of the dryer, then why don't you tell me what you found out at work?''

''Why don't you want to be with me tonight?'' he countered. As if she wouldn't know what he meant, he clarified by adding, ''Sexually, Peggy.''

He definitely cut right to the chase. No doubt about it, she thought, the man was a professional profiler. ''What?'' She raised an eyebrow. ''Do you read minds?''

''Of course.''

''It's a tense time right now,'' she ventured.

''And that's why you're afraid of me?''

''I'm afraid of Miles McLaughlin and Susan Jones,'' she corrected.

''You fear me more.''

Once more, he was right on target. Before she could respond, one of his big, sexy hands was in her hair. His fingers, spread wide apart, traced her temple, then pushed back the strands; like a comb against her scalp, his fingertips felt so dreamily good that Peggy couldn't help but sigh and surrender, letting the force of his touch drive her head backward. As if his fingers had tugged the cord to a window blind, her eyes shuttered, too. Before her eyelashes parted again, Oliver took the advantage. Just as his mouth covered hers, she whispered, ''Oliver, I mean it, really...''

But it was too late. His mouth was moving on hers. She'd meant the words, but ever since their first night together, he'd engendered an unforgettable bodily craving. ''It's the wrong time for me to start a relationship,'' she murmured against his mouth. ''Maybe after this is all over, maybe when we know I'm safe…''

But he probably knew the truth. When he leaned back a fraction to survey her, she could see that. If he let her go now, she'd fight the physical pull and intellectualize the animal hunger that bound them. So, he simply took her mouth again, whispering, ''Does this have to be a relationship?''

''What else could it be?''

He chuckled softly. ''Great sex.''

Maybe he had a point. Without responding, she let him kiss her again, this time more deeply and with more heat. Not because he overpowered her. Or because he forced her to surrender. But because she wanted him so desperately.

As his hand stroked her side, sensuality burst inside her, and as he stretched his tongue to explore hers, hers met his. When he pressed forward again, she shuddered from the feel of his erection, the thin fabric of her dress and his trousers no barrier to their bodies. He was straining, so obviously wanting her that her mind darkened, her senses careening, seemingly into nowhere.

When he reached wordlessly and grabbed her hand, tugging her toward the bedroom, she was ready. He'd infused every cell with desire. And by the time they reached the water bed, any logical thought had vanished from her mind. Somewhere far off was a crazy world of danger that had little to do with simple Peggy Fox, flight attendant, who shared an apartment with four other women, and who worked hard, and worried over her mother and Aunt Jill in Ohio.

Somewhere far off was that horrible moment in the Rainbow Room when she'd accepted a faux-diamond engagement ring from a man who didn't really love her—and whose real girlfriend was a criminal. And there was a felon named Susan Jones who had actually aimed a weapon at Peggy and fired.

Somewhere far off, nicer things were happening, too. Couples were buying a first Christmas tree together. Church choirs were caroling. Kids were sitting on Santa's lap while they told him what they wanted in their stockings.

But all those things seemed a million miles away. All that mattered was right here. This man who was pulling her dress over her head. Simultaneously, Oliver shrugged out of his jacket. His eyes never left hers as he unknotted his tie, then unbuttoned his shirt. With one roll of his powerful shoulders, the shirt hit the floor. The pants followed. As the briefs came down, she valiantly tried to pull in a quick breath, but the air couldn't quite make it to her lungs. Oliver was thoroughly aroused, his skin flushed with heat.

He noticed the panties, too. "Nice," he muttered throatily, sliding a finger along the slit in the fabric. "Red. My favorite color."

"Last night you said your favorite color was blue."

He smiled. "Changed my mind."

She smiled back. "When?"

"Right this very second, Peggy."

Slowly, he glided the finger back and forth, then he changed directions and pressed the finger inward...deep inside her. A second finger followed. Each time he withdrew, he twisted his hand, sending fire rippling through her. "I take it Kiki put these in the duffel."

She nodded, her heart hammering. "Yeah."

"I think we'll leave them on."

She arched for his touch as his thumb glided over her clitoris. Somehow, she found her voice. "I thought you might like them."

The words he murmured against her ear were husky. "That would be an understatement, Peg."

Peg. He'd never called her that. Her mind growing hazy with the sensations of his touch, she reached down, and using the backs of both hands, stroked his thighs until he moaned. "Touch me, too," he whispered.

As her hand closed around his shaft, she released a sigh. There was so much of Oliver. He was so big. Squeezing as she glided a hand up and down, she let his growing excitement—the involuntary thrust of his hips and flex of his erection—drive her toward the edge. The work of his fingers pushed her closer to the brink. Oblivion seemed within reach as she slipped her hand lower, panting softly as she found his balls. Gently weighing them in her hands, she bounced lightly, registering their tightness until he caught her hand.

"C'mon," he said raggedly, urging her onto the bed, using her hip to turn her onto her side.

He didn't follow, not yet, but merely stared down at her for a moment. The window blinds were drawn, but shafts of light from the streetlamps sliced through the slats and illuminated his face. "You're beautiful," he said, his voice barely audible as if words were failing him because what they'd just shared was already more than he could take. "Cameron," he added huskily. "You really are her, you know."

As aroused as she felt, it was hard to muster a smile, but she did. "In what way?"

"I can't imagine a sexier woman in America."

"I can't imagine a sexier man."

"Condoms are never sexy," he said, and as he took one from the bedside table, she realized his hand was shaking. That's how badly he wanted her.

"They're sexy right now," she said, shuddering as he rolled one downward and pinched the tip. He slid next to her on the bed, and despite his readiness, he cupped her face with his hands and stared into her eyes, the long, unbroken connection more intimate that anything she'd ever known. And then he kissed her languidly, as if he had all the time in the world until they were both moaning, wanting more.

Finally he leaned back, looking downward between their bodies as he arched his back, thrusting into the red slit. His weight rolled with the bed. An answering wave of water caught her hips and propelled her to him. Each stroke brought a new wave she could ride to shore, and each time their hips reunited, she felt herself frothing, like a breaker on sand. Something deep inside her was about to shatter, she knew. His eyes were so full of hunger. They were heavily lidded, and his parted lips emitted ragged breaths. "Cameron," he whispered.

"Let me be your fantasy woman," she whispered back as they rode the waves. "What would you like to do with me?"

Already, the sex was too hot to last. He drove

deeper, harder. Slick and hot, she was taking all of him. "Only this."

Full and aching, her breasts met his harder chest, and the peaking tips brushed back and forth against a black pelt of swirling hair. Feeling jittery with need and ready for ecstasy, she glanced down, too, and now her thighs opened farther at the sight of him...*down there*. Throbbing, he vanished inside the panties.

Skin and lace, she thought vaguely, the naughtiness of it sending another thrill through her—one that brought her hips off the mattress. *Red panties... skin...lace...*

It was too much now. When another undulating wave pushed him back inside, he went so deep that she cried out. Greedily, his mouth fell to her neck, and he didn't so much kiss as drink. "Now," he uttered hoarsely. They came together. Explosive and swift, the mutual satisfaction seemed strangely unbelievable.

"Usually that doesn't happen," she managed to say a few moments later, when the pulsing of her body had almost subsided.

He knew what she meant. "No, it doesn't," he whispered between kisses as he pulled her on top of him, into his arms. "Did it change your mind about not wanting involvements?"

Why did he have to bring that up now? Her heart was only beginning to still. She breathed in, then out, very slowly. "I...need time to sort things out."

"We can keep it casual."

"All right."

But it was a lie. Just a little white lie, she thought.

The kind of heat they shared could never be casual. Sighing, she stared through the window. Between the slats of the closed blind, she could see slivers of the night sky and catch glimpses of the nightclub across the street. The snow was falling in sheets. On the ground, it was at least a foot deep, maybe more.

She didn't know how much time passed before he said, "This might turn into another snowstorm like the one we had back in the late nineties, remember?"

She chuckled, loving the feel of her lips grazing his chest hairs. "Yeah. You couldn't drive. Not even cabs were allowed to use the streets."

"The city was…" He lowered his voice to a whisper. "Really quiet."

She laughed softly. "And kids were everywhere." Her finger stilled where it had been tracing circles on his chest. She tried to push away the thought, but she was imagining having kids…with this man.

"The city's different from Ohio, huh?"

"Very. How about Utah?"

"Very."

A long silence fell, then she said, "Do you think we'll have a white Christmas, Oliver."

His voice was husky. "Yeah."

"Do you think we'll be together on Christmas?"

He shrugged. "Do you mind?"

She considered. "Not really," she finally admitted. "I miss Mom and Aunt Jill, but…" As her voice trailed off, she vaguely realized her plans to back off from the relationship hadn't really materialized. "You?"

"I don't mind," he said. "And who knows? Maybe we'll figure something out before then."

Feeling relieved for the change in topic, she snuggled on top of him. "What did you find out at work?"

"Plenty. Definitely enough to connect Miles to Susan Jones. There's no undercover sting. Those two go way back. Miles was the first person to interview Susan after she was arrested for her first bank job. He was also the person responsible for getting her parole. As near as I can tell, he produced documentation saying he'd used her as a snitch."

"He didn't?"

"I doubt it."

Before Oliver could elaborate, Miles McLaughlin's voice broke through the silence. They both started, then Oliver urged her from his chest, rose from bed and headed for the living room. Grabbing a chenille throw that had been folded near the footboard, Peggy swirled it around her shoulders and followed Oliver with Midnight scampering on her heels.

When she reached the recording machine in the living room, Oliver tilted the earphone toward her and she cocked her head, listening. Hearing Miles's voice was bad enough, but then Susan Jones purred, "I got the tickets, baby." Peggy would know that voice anywhere. It was the same one that had demanded of Miles, "What's she doing here?"

"Assumed names?" asked Miles.

"Of course. We're traveling as Mortimer and Sally Fife. I got a haircut and picked up some red dye for myself, and I picked up a brown wig and mustache for you." She sighed. "In just a few days, your life is going to change."

Peggy hoped so. She hoped she and Oliver managed to put Miles and Susan in jail. Peggy pursed her lips as Miles's voice sounded. "Ah." He sighed. "No more meetings. No more lousy government paychecks. When do we leave?"

"The day after Christmas."

"Airport security's going to be tighter then."

"True," Susan Jones returned, "but we'll also be able to get lost in the crowd. It's the year's heaviest day for airline travel."

"We shouldn't meet until then."

"I'll call and tell you where." Susan paused. "Have you heard anything about…"

"No," he said. "Nothing."

Peggy tensed, wondering if they'd been referring to her, and praying they wouldn't say anything to alert Oliver to her and Miles's affair. Given that Susan had nearly killed her in what had seemed a fit of jealousy, it stood to reason that Susan knew about the false engagement. Suddenly, Peggy shivered. It still seemed so incredible. Had she nearly been murdered by a jealous woman? Had she really been part of a dangerous love triangle?

For a second, the warmth of Christmas seemed far away, and New York felt too cold for a small-town girl such as herself. Sighing, she wondered if she should come clean—and tell Oliver that she'd actually fallen for the wrong man, and that it wasn't the first time.

My life, she thought simply. She was going to have to talk to Oliver again about ending their affair. Maybe that was the more pressing issue. She needed to straighten out her romantic experiences. After Miles and Susan rang off, she looked at Oliver. "Where do you think they're going?"

Oliver shrugged, looking delectable, since he was wearing no clothes. "I don't know." He frowned. "I'm sure they used secure phone lines, but maybe not. I can check tomorrow. He was working late, and she called him at the office." Oliver absently chewed his bottom lip. "At least this is proof that our assumptions are right. He's leaving town with her. With any luck, I'll be able to trace the call."

"And if not?" Peggy was trying to keep her gaze fixed on his upper body, but it kept trailing downward.

He shrugged again. "Hopefully, we'll catch another phone call. Next time, maybe they'll name the destination, and I can be on the flight."

She'd like nothing more than to confront Miles. "Sounds good." Suddenly, she gasped. "The casserole! It was in the microwave!"

A smile lifted Oliver's lips. "Great. What say we have dinner in bed?"

Peggy thought back to the Washington Square Hotel. "It won't be the first time."

He chuckled. "But this time, it'll be a lot easier."

Squinting, she found herself enjoying—and returning—his easy laughter. Despite the fact that they'd just overheard a conversation between two felons, one of whom had tried to shoot her, she felt safe, even happy. "Easier?"

Oliver grasped her hand, twining his fingers with hers and heading for the kitchen. "Uh-huh. Because this time, you're not wearing those Lycra pants."

Just before he turned, caught her in an embrace and settled his mouth on hers once more, she whispered, "Admit it, Oliver. You loved those Lycra pants."

10

"C'MON," OLIVER SAID a few days later, glancing over his shoulder and tugging Peggy's hand as they went up the stairs to the roof of Anna's building. "It's Christmas Eve. Let's enjoy it."

How could she? Mustering a smile, she thrust her hands deeply into the pockets of a navy pea coat she'd found in the living-room closet, sighing as she located a pair of knit gloves. The truth was, each moment she spent with Oliver was making her feel more confused. Mostly because she'd never felt as happy as during the past few days. When Oliver was at work, she was conscious of feeling a burning craving for him, and while she'd never imagined herself watching the clock, waiting for a man to come home, she found herself doing so now.

Every day, they'd get naked within the first few minutes of his arrival, too. It was a novelty. Peggy had never had a man come home to her at all, much less hungry for sex. And Oliver made her feel great about herself sexually. They'd just spent the past two hours making love, and she was still flying high. He always encouraged her to touch him in new ways...

At times, she didn't even remember the real reason why she was here. Anna and Vic's home seemed like a dream haven, a place out of time. Between the heavy snowfall and the quiet that had fallen since so many people left New York for Christmas, the apartment felt less like a city dwelling and more like an isolated cottage in the woods.

Peggy sighed again. Not an hour ago, she'd been lying in front of a fire, on the faux-bearskin rug with Oliver, letting him bathe every inch of her with spine-tingling kisses while the red glow cast from the chili-pepper lights on the Christmas tree danced on his skin. Their physical rapport was amazing. Shouldn't this be leading to something more? she wondered now. It seemed so special.

And yet she wasn't ready for more, was she? Recently, she'd been drawn in by Miles McLaughlin, proving beyond a doubt that her internal radar was buggy when it came to men. What if she'd accidentally married someone such as that? What if such a man became the father of her children? Or what if her mistake wasn't quite so devastating as that? What if she simply made the same mistake as her mom and Aunt Jill—and wound up alone? Being betrayed one too many times, and giving up on male-female relationships altogether?

She shook her head as if to clear it of confusion. Days had passed, and while two more calls had come through on the recorder, Miles and Susan hadn't yet risked divulging their destination. More and more, Oliver was considering whether to take this case to his superiors, but he feared if Miles had contacts, he might be alerted. Tomorrow would be Peggy's first Christmas without her mom and Aunt Jill, too. She'd talked to them on the phone, and thankfully no one had yet mentioned seeing Peggy on TV, but she missed them.

"Sorry," she suddenly murmured, feeling winded as they reached the fifth floor. "I just wish we'd figured out where Miles and Susan are going." Since Oliver wasn't sure if Kevin Hall was aware of Miles's relationship with Susan, he'd decided not to take the information to other New York–based agents.

"There's still time. If we haven't heard anything by the day after Christmas, I'll call Ohringer. He's trustworthy." Ohringer was his boss in Quantico. "I know he couldn't be involved, and he can alert officials at airports, at least."

"Miles and Susan will be in disguise," she pointed out.

"True. But maybe somebody will recognize them."

When they reached the top of the stairs, Oliver pulled her against his chest, then turned so that her back was pressed against the heavy metal door that led onto the roof.

"Trapping me?" she asked huskily.

He smiled. "Looks that way."

She smiled back. "Feels that way, too, Oliver."

"Then I guess it is that way," he said as she lifted her chin for the kiss. At nothing more than the touch of their lips, her whole body started melting. The cold winter air seeping through the door only made her that much more aware of the warmth gliding through her veins. Like the wind, it seemed to race inside her, whistling around bones and sinews and blowing itself into her extremities.

Threading her fingers into his hair, she pulled him closer, increasing the pressure of his mouth until every erogenous zone ached. She arched against him, and when she found it was pointless because of the bulk of their coats, frustration left her feeling bothered and edgy. Her eyes fluttered shut as he cupped her neck, his long fingers stroking, then circling it.

"Looks like this promises to be good," he murmured, gliding an index finger along her skin.

"Feels good," she whispered.

He chuckled. "Guess it *is* good, then."

"You'll have to taste to make sure. Now, won't you, Oliver?"

"Guess so." His thumb caught beneath her chin, and he tilted back her head again before nuzzling inside the collar of her coat and licking an unbroken line of kisses from her collarbone to her ear. Slowly, he swirled his tongue around the shell, dipped inside, then blew on the spots he'd left wet, making her shiver.

"Tastes like everything that looking at you promises."

"I don't break promises."

Given the soft pant of his breath and the barely discernible tremor in his finger as he traced her jaw, it was clear he wanted more. "Is that so?"

"Maybe we should go back inside," she said, leaning back a fraction so she could look up into his eyes.

"Now, now," he chided, his expression distracted as if he was thinking of the past few hours during which they'd pleasured each other. "I thought we agreed it was time to get out of bed and take a look at the outside world for a change."

"You've kept me hostage so long I'm not sure I can still appreciate Mother Nature," she teased throatily. "I'm afraid I've become a shut-in."

"Isolated, huh?"

"Very."

"But not alone," he said, his eyes sparkling with mischief.

Her lips upturned. "I've had some company," she admitted.

He grinned. "Even I like to free my hostages occasionally."

"What a pity," she whispered. "I'm not sure I'm really ready for this outside world of yours."

"Not to worry—" His voice lowered with desire. "You'll be safe up here. Besides, I'm not sure a rooftop in Greenwich Village really qualifies as Mother Nature."

"Ah," she murmured as he used a finger to brush back the lock of recalcitrant hair that was always falling over her eye. "I see. You're slowly breaking me in…introducing me to nature by gradual degrees. We're starting with nature on a small scale. And building up to *Mother* Nature."

"Exactly. That's my strategy." Once more, he settled a thumb on her chin and lifted her face, tilting up her mouth so that he could easily take it. "Now, when it comes to nature," he schooled, "body heat comes first."

Impulsively, she stretched on her tiptoes and

claimed his mouth again. "Sex next," she agreed. "And then?"

"You say that as if I should have a game plan after that."

"Do you?"

"Usually, I'm spontaneous, as you may have noticed, but when it comes to your nature lesson, I don't mind telling you that I'm saving the lions, tigers and bears for last."

She emitted a mock gasp. "I didn't know you were into bestiality!"

He laughed. "That's not what I meant, and you know it."

She merely kissed him again, planting a quick, puckered-lip smooch on his mouth, then she frowned. "So, there won't be any bears up on the roof?" she asked, liking the banter they so easily shared. "I'm crushed, Ollie. You promised to entertain me."

"Oh, I'll entertain you," he assured. Coming closer, he squinted at her. "Usually, I only let my little sister get away with calling me Ollie," he added.

Before she thought it through, she said, "I'm not special enough?"

For a heartbeat, the question hovered, then his lips were on hers once more, feeling cool and firm at first, then warming like a slow-building fire. He murmured, "You're special, all right. Really special, Peg."

She swallowed hard, knowing she'd fished for that response, and knowing she did—and didn't—want to hear it. "C'mon," she said a bit too brightly, "last one outside's a rotten egg."

"*You're* challenging *me?*" Oliver twisted his lips

into a bemused grin, then he placed his hands on her shoulders and simply, forcibly, removed her from in front of the door.

"Ladies first," she said on a guffaw.

"Fat chance."

She was still laughing as he made a point of turning away and flinging open the door. Icy blasts of air gusted inside as he crossed the threshold. Staring across the flat roof, she could see that the snow was still coming down hard, sweeping in almost impenetrable gusts like a hard rain. A second after Oliver began jogging toward the ledge overlooking the street, he became nearly invisible.

"The ghost of Oliver." As Peggy whispered the words, something inside her wrenched at the thought of ever losing him. Quickly pushing aside the feeling, she tugged on the knit gloves. Anna's boots were a size too large, so Peggy found herself smiling again when she nearly stumbled, lurching across the threshold. Her feet sank into white powder, and when she plowed forward, she felt as if she were slugging through wet sand.

Using her shoulder, she pushed the door shut against the wind. "I can't believe this," she muttered, voicing more frustration than she actually felt as she headed for Oliver, her heels furrowing through the snow.

"It's beautiful out here," she said when she caught up to him. He'd placed both hands on a ledge and was leaning over it, staring down onto Barrow Street.

Just as she threw her arms around his waist and squeezed, he reversed their positions, so that he was standing behind her with his hands clasped across her belly. Resting her forearms over his, she twined their fingers and glanced over her shoulder, smiling.

He smiled back. "Yeah," he agreed. "It's pretty. Looks like a country road down there."

She took in the strip of roadway, unmarked by tire tracks, then her gaze swept the rest of the terrain, including the chimney tops and the neat rows of brick and stone tenements surrounding them. Snow blanketed every inch. Not even parked cars below were visible, and the roofs of buildings looked good enough to eat, as if they'd been heavily iced with melting marshmallow frosting. Windowsills and gargoyles on cornices were all white-encrusted.

Under the soft yellow light emitted from streetlamps and apartment windows, the snow on the ground looked as fine as fairy dust. Crystals sparkled against the white, causing her to say, "It looks like glitter."

He leaned in closer, holding her tightly against him, his cheek feeling cool next to hers. "Yeah," he said in an almost whisper, "it sure does."

"Cold out here, though."

"You need a man to warm you up."

"I have a man."

"You do?" he teased.

She hesitated. "For the moment." Before he could respond, she pointedly added, "It *was* warmer in bed."

"You can't get your mind off it, can you?"

"What?"

"Having sex with me."

Again, that unwanted knot lodged in her throat. Her mind whirled, as fast as a flurry in this wind, and she wondered what was really happening between them. Keeping her tone light, she finally said, ''It was fun.''

''Is,'' he corrected, nuzzling kisses on her cheek. ''We'll be making love again soon enough.''

Making love.

She stiffened, reacting to the ease with which he'd said the phrase. She and Oliver were getting so close; she should have stood her ground and backed off from the relationship. And yet, despite the thought, she continued leaning against him, enjoying the coiled strength in his tall, lean body and the feeling of hard male muscles pressing against each inch of her back.

Shuddering, she realized they were like teenagers who couldn't keep their hands off each other. Night after night, she'd lain in his arms, doing exactly what he'd just said—making love. A shiver grazed down her spine, more from memories of hot sex than from the cold. And then she felt a spark of anger. Earlier tonight, she'd read a copy of Miles's personnel file, which Oliver had stolen—or, as he put it, ''temporarily borrowed''—from the human resources office at work.

The contents had infuriated her. Practically everything Miles had told her about his personal background was a lie. He hadn't had a happy family life, for instance. In reality, his parents were divorced, just as hers were, and he hadn't continued a relationship with his father, as she hadn't. Nor had he gone to an Ivy League university as he'd claimed. He'd barely graduated with grades good enough to get him into the FBI.

Small white lies weren't what she'd expected to find, somehow. Because Oliver had said people like Miles had often been hurt in childhood, Peggy had half expected to discover horrible stories—that Miles had been abused, somehow, but as near as Peggy could tell, Miles's background was on a par with hers. So, why had Miles turned out to be a liar and a thief?

The profile Oliver had written about Miles didn't shed much light on the matter. According to Oliver, Miles really was a narcissistic personality, though. The bureau had more than a few. Often, people who'd sustained damage to their sense of self could make exemplary employees. Needing to prove themselves, they frequently excelled. Their shaky self-esteem couldn't take failure, and it made them go the extra mile.

Especially in bed, Oliver had argued. Guys like Miles couldn't live without a number of women to bolster his flagging self-concept. He was the type to surround himself with many. Which meant Peggy had been simply one more notch in his belt.

"A penny," Oliver murmured.

She realized he was watching her carefully. "I was thinking about your profile of Miles McLaughlin," she said honestly.

He arched a dark eyebrow. "And?"

She shrugged. "I was thinking about how you said he liked to use women...to feel his power over them."

"He likes to feel they'll love him despite his

wrongdoings,'' added Oliver. ''Getting away with something bad is proof that he really is loved. The more he's forgiven, the more powerful he feels. He pushes the envelope with people. Eventually, he'll double-cross Susan Jones.''

''Take the money from her heist for himself?''

''That or bring another woman home.''

Peggy's cheeks burned despite the cold. How could she have been so blind? So stupid?

''He'll want to see the women interact,'' Oliver continued, oblivious of her thoughts. ''He'll want to know who's angriest. Who loves him the most. Who fights for him.''

That would be Susan Jones. She'd nearly killed Peggy over the worst kind of man imaginable. Abruptly, propelled by a knee-jerk reaction, Peggy pulled Oliver's hands from her waist. ''C'mon,'' she muttered, circling him and heading toward the door.

She was ten paces away before she realized she shouldn't have moved, since Oliver would probably ask her for an explanation. She could almost see him standing behind her, his lips pursed in surprise, his eyes narrowed in confusion. Maybe she didn't care, she decided. She needed time and space—not another man's seamless seductions.

His voice sounded behind her. ''Where are you going?''

''Inside.''

Just as she reached the door and pulled it open, he caught her shoulder and turned her to face him. ''Peg,'' he said, his expression just as she'd imagined, his dark eyes squinting in concern. "What's going on? What just happened?"

Suddenly, she was aware that her heart was pounding too hard in her chest. *Quit looking at me that way,* she thought. Maybe she would have said it, but her mouth felt too dry. Besides, she was too moved by the tenderness in his eyes, a tenderness that made it tempting to tell him that she'd been on cloud nine when Miles McLaughlin had asked her to marry him. Now that another man was interested in her, that was somehow easier to admit, but it still hurt. She'd been so impressed by Miles, so taken in by his supposed accomplishments and job title, and his talk of all the high-profile crimes he'd solved.

She'd thought, foolish small-town girl that she was, that maybe roughing it with four other young women while they tried to make it in the big city had finally paid off, and that her dreams were coming true. Yes, she'd been so impressed with him, just as she'd been impressed by Oliver. He, too, was handsome and accomplished, and she wasn't about to trust her instincts again. "I just want to go inside," she managed to say. "Okay?"

"No. It's not okay."

Right now, he was every bit the psychologist; that was the worst thing. He was using that soft, gentle, coaxing tone. And his eyes were encouraging and patient.

"Just give me a minute," she said.

But he made no move to back away. The hand on her shoulder moved downward, closing around her upper arm. At that moment, his sheer physical presence felt overwhelming. The heat of his breath was too enticing; the scent of his body too arousing.

"Why did thinking about Miles make you bolt, Peg?"

She felt as if he was able to see right through her. "It wasn't Miles."

"It was."

"Don't you ever back off?"

"Not when it comes to what I want."

She eyed him with exasperation. "What do you want?"

"You."

"Whatever happened to keeping things casual?"

He didn't bother to answer, but merely pulled her against him, the unexpected movement almost rough, the fingers he threaded into her hair an obvious precursor to a kiss that never came.

"Let's try one more time," he said. "What's going on?"

She exhaled a shaky breath. She had to trust him a little bit, didn't she? "I've had a lot of trouble with men."

"That would make you a woman." His eyes flicked between hers and the lips she'd parted slightly for that phantom kiss. "I've never met one who *hasn't* had trouble with men, Peg. We're trouble."

"*You* definitely are," she couldn't help but say dryly. Then she blew out another annoyed breath that fogged the air between them. "My boyfriends haven't been what..." Pausing, she searched for the right words and settled on, "What I need."

Oliver looked very interested. "What you need?"

She nodded. "Emotionally."

"Dammit," he muttered, "I can be emotional, Peg. You're the one who didn't want to get involved, who said she just wanted sex."

"And I do want sex. Or I did."

He looked hurt. "You don't now?"

This conversation was definitely heading in the wrong direction. Suddenly, she glanced around. All at once, unexpected tears were pushing against her eyelids, since she had absolutely no idea what she wanted, not from him or any man. "I just need to think things over and start making sure I'm working toward the relationships that will make me happiest. When you choose a partner, it can be a choice you make for life…"

Her voice trailed off. This was getting worse by the minute. Why was she talking as if she and Oliver might be making a choice for life?

His eyes had turned more assessing. So softly that she almost didn't hear him, he said, "Who screwed you over, sweetheart?"

She considered. "A lot of people, actually," she finally admitted. "A guy named Gerald Slater used my ATM card and withdrew some spending money. In order to pay my bills that month, I had to work double shifts. Then a guy named Steven Winkler used my phone to call 1–900 numbers."

Oliver was staring at her in disbelief. "He was your boyfriend?"

"Well, not really. I hadn't slept with him." Yet. But she'd been about to, not that Oliver needed that piece of information.

Oliver merely nodded. "You were on a date?"

She knew her cheeks were scarlet. "Yeah. I had gone around the corner to get some take-out for us when he made the calls. He said he wanted to stay inside and watch the game." She paused, then added, "He'd been watching a Pittsburgh team play Miami."

"And when did this happen?"

Oliver's physical closeness was still making her insides quake, and she suddenly wished they could forget the whole conversation and just start kissing again. "When I was in college."

"College was a long time ago, Peggy."

She was as sensitive as the next female to comments about her age. "Not that long ago," she defended.

"You know what I mean."

She guessed she did. "But it didn't stop in college. For instance, Kiki introduced me to someone she met on a first-class European flight—a guy named Groucho Garfield."

"Groucho?"

"That's the point. It wasn't his name, after all. According to his identification cards, he was Samson Anderson."

"And you got his identification cards by…"

"They were in his jacket pocket."

"And Samson Anderson was…"

"In the bathroom at the time." Samson Anderson had been in there a suspiciously long time, too, not that she was going to tell Oliver. She had absolutely no idea what Samson Anderson had been doing in there. And she did not want to know.

Oliver was looking as if she was becoming more fascinating by the second, and she wasn't sure how she felt about that, either. No woman in her right mind would dislike being the object of this dark-eyed intelligent stare, and yet she was starting to feel as if he was profiling her again, digging beneath the surface, trying to find out what made her tick.

"Dating is difficult," he finally said.

"A lot of people are weird," she agreed. "My roommate Isabella met an out-of-work Web site developer on the Internet who sent her a singing male stripper the very next day."

"Interesting," he said. Then there was a long pause before he added, "Are you in the habit of looking through dates' wallets?"

Probably, he was thinking of her looking through his wallet at the Washington Square Hotel. "You can never be too careful," she said. "I've learned the hard way."

"But these men sound inconsequential, Peggy."

True. But Miles hadn't been. She hadn't felt for him what she did for Oliver Vargo, of course. There'd been none of this bodily hunger and insistent, undeniable craving for sex. She'd never felt restless frustration as she waited for him to get off work and come home.

But she'd been unforgivably gullible. Overly impressed and dangerously unable to see through him. Just as her mother hadn't seen through Peggy's father, and her Aunt Jill hadn't seen through *her* husband. Oliver was exactly right. Those other men had been inconsequential, and fortunately, her blind spot for trouble hadn't resulted in any irreversible situation. Death, however, was irreversible. And with Miles McLaughlin, her blind spot had become nearly deadly.

She could almost hear the gears in Oliver's mind churning. "Please," she said, hoping to head off any psychologizing. "Don't tell me my father's abandonment has made me unable to trust men."

"Has it?"

"Of course."

Gazing into his gorgeous brown eyes, she couldn't help but wonder if she'd like living with a man who had degrees in psychology. Surprisingly, a sense of safety washed over her. Would Oliver be the kind of man with whom she could share all her troubles? All her secrets? Should she change her mind? Risk it— and tell him about Miles? And yet…it was as if by telling him, she'd be letting him in all the way. But by keeping secrets…

Catching the drift of her thoughts, she turned abruptly and reached for the door, but his fingers only tightened around her arm. "Not so fast."

She faced him. "You want me to go slow?"

"Real slow." Just as she registered how husky his voice had become, Oliver leaned closer.

And then his mouth was on hers once more. There was just no stopping the man. He was insatiable.

"IT'S BEEN A GREAT Christmas," Oliver murmured the next night, pulling her closer against him as he rolled over in bed, his heated naked body pressed against her back, so that they spooned together, allowing him to enter her from behind.

"You feel so good," she whispered shakily, sighing as he drove inside, letting her enjoy the burn of each inch. He didn't rest until his pelvic bone was pressed against her backside.

Together, they shuddered. He flexed inside her as he glided his hands upward on her belly, her skin feeling as smooth as the red-and-green satin sheets he'd bought for the bed. From beneath, he lifted both breasts. He was impossibly hard already, but further stiffened inside her as he touched her. She was so beautiful, so perfect. Curling his fingers, he cupped the undersides of her breasts, then reached up... up...up...until he could strum nipples as hard as he felt enveloped in her moist, fiery heat.

She was wearing a Santa hat he'd seen previously in the drugstore. "You've been naughty," he whispered hoarsely, reading the message scrawled in red on the white brim.

"Maybe I need a spanking."

Oliver's chest tightened as he gave up fondling a breast, just long enough to ease away from her, loving how she gasped over each inch of his withdrawal. Slipping a hand between them, he curved it over her backside, then using his palm, he rubbed slow brisk circles there, sensitizing the skin. When it was good and warm, he gave her a love tap that drew a cry— not of pain, but of pleasure.

"Nice," she corrected on a pant, reaching up and turning the brim to the side that said, "I've been nice."

His ragged breath was the only response. His arms crossed her torso, his left closing loosely over her right breast, his right traveling downward toward the hot flesh between her legs. Suddenly, he felt he'd never be able to hold her close enough.

"Ah," he managed to whisper as his finger teased, flicking the nub. Catching her moisture, he rubbed circles around her clitoris. Meantime, the splayed fingers of his left hand were playing games, too, circling her breast, cupping it completely, so that the nipple rested against the hollow of his palm. With excruciating slowness, he drew his fingers upward, stroking her breast so lightly that each finger could have been a strand of silk.

Last night, she'd scared him. He'd realized he didn't want Peggy Fox to leave his life. He'd felt the same way this morning. Knowing she shouldn't go out, she'd thought ahead to Christmas. At some point, probably the first day she'd arrived, she'd ordered a chair from L. L. Bean that matched the hammock in his yard at Quantico.

"How did you know I had a hammock?" he'd asked, surprised.

She'd merely grinned in a way that made his heart do crazy flip-flops. "It was in the picture in the back of your book," she'd said. "You know, next to your bio."

Not that he hadn't been thoughtful, too. He'd gotten her a blue silk robe. And, of course, the Santa hat. After they'd opened their gifts, they'd called their families. And then he'd quizzed Peggy, reading choice excerpts from the Sex Files, which had just been released.

When he'd asked her to guess the penis size of the average male, she'd actually found a tape measure and measured him. "Above average," she'd pronounced.

By then, he'd been hard as a rock, and laughing, they'd tumbling into bed where they'd been ever since. The day had seemed so…perfect. Whatever her relational problems, Oliver had found himself wishing that Anna and Vic's place was really a home they shared. He wanted to bind Peggy to him, so that she'd never want to go home. Realizing he was close to the edge, he held back as she started to buck against him.

Over and over, he stroked her breast, circling it with his loosely held fingers, then drawing his fingers slowly upward toward the nipple. As he caught the turgid tip firmly between his fingers and thumb, she cried out. Pinching, he tugged, pulling the nipple as he worked it in ever slower circles.

Begging him, she whispered, "Please…please…"

"If you've been nice," he said on a pant, "then maybe Santa will give you something you want for Christmas. What do you want?"

The word sounded strangled. "This."

"This? Me doing what to you, sweetheart?"

She uttered what was usually an oath. Something unprintable that described what he was doing to her…and what she wanted him to do. "Do it, Oliver…"

Gliding his hands, so they molded over her hips, he braced himself, his backside tightening. Suddenly, he arched, pulling her to him as his rigid length slid into her waiting flesh again. He went deep, his whole body shaking from pleasure and the iron-willed control that kept him on the edge of climax.

His mind jumbled. Last night, he'd brought her to bed and loved her as much as he could. Yeah. She'd scared him on the roof. She'd turned and bolted without explanation, the sudden move taking him by surprise. Now he stroked between her legs—harder, faster. But he didn't make it. He couldn't hold out. His own orgasm was too sudden, too overwhelming. But it was all right. She was gushing, and the tiny internal spasms felt like heaven. *Don't go home, Peg,* he wanted to say as he buried his face against her shoulder.

But he didn't.

HOURS LATER, the phone recorder picked up.

"We're all set for tomorrow," Susan said. "I'm glad you're at the office, Miles. I didn't think you'd be there."

He sounded terse. "Then why'd you call?"

"I tried you at home, but…"

"Like I said, the office is the only place that gets swept regularly for bugs. Besides, I forgot to wipe out some of my computer files. On Christmas night, I knew no one would be here." He sighed. "You know that guy I told you about? Vargo?"

"Yes."

"I don't trust him. I looked through some of the stuff on his desk, and I think he may be checking me out. There was a piece of paper with my name on it."

"Well, it doesn't matter. We're leaving tomorrow. You'll never have to think about him again. Are you sure you're okay with going to Paris?"

"It's a starting point. After we're safely outside the U.S., we can go anywhere. We'll have to. Basically, once we pick up the money, we should be somewhere else within twenty-four hours."

"The money? Are you sure you can get it out?"

He laughed confidently. "Earlier today, I used my credentials to ship it. With so many people thinking about the holidays, nobody was suspicious. Everybody thinks I'm shipping out French-made counterfeit dollars. Because no one thinks the money's real, they won't watch it as closely on transport."

Susan sounded worried. "How do we pick it up?"

"An American courier named Mortimer Fife, who'll be traveling with his wife, Sally, will pick up the money. Supposedly, he's an agent who'll transport it to the authorities. I faxed my picture, dressed in the disguise I'll be wearing."

"Brilliant," whispered Susan. There was a sudden catch in her voice. "I can't wait to see you, Miles. Tomorrow at noon, at the gate, right? I've missed you so much."

"Missed you, too."

But he didn't sound sincere, Oliver decided. "I bet Miles will leave her as soon as he's got the money," he said to Peggy when the call was over.

"What do we do now?"

Oliver phoned for flight information. "Judging from what they said," he announced as he recradled the receiver, "they've got to be leaving on a 12:20

flight. And—" he sent her a long, sideways glance "—as it turns out, the Fifes are booked on your airline."

Relief flooded her features. "That's usually Sophie's flight, but she may have tried to take off for the holidays. It's possible that she got Juliette or Isabella to trade with her. I thought Kiki was scheduled for a bicoastal." She paused. "Well, I'll call them. If one of them's not an attendant, they'll know who is. Or be able to find out for us by noon tomorrow."

Oliver could only stare. "And you need this information because…?"

"So I can be on the flight."

"I was afraid of that."

Peggy looked confused. "We have to be on it, right?"

"I do. You don't. You're not going."

"Am, too." Before he could protest, Peggy grasped his waist and pulled him onto the living-room couch—on top of her.

"Maybe so," Oliver found himself murmuring. "Because you can be very hard to argue with, Peggy Fox."

11

"I WONDER if you'll be able to catch Ohringer at home," Peggy said an hour later, sliding her fingers over the back of Oliver's hand and lifting it from the phone receiver before he could call his boss at Quantico. Getting Oliver to let her come with him was going to be difficult; once he involved the agency, she'd be left in New York unless he convinced his superiors otherwise.

He shrugged. "I figure he'll be home tonight. He's got grown kids, both married, and they usually come in for the holidays. By now, their children will be in bed, and the adults will probably be talking. I know they were planning their usual family get-together this year. He and his wife even invited me for Christmas dinner."

"That was nice."

"Yeah. He knew Anna and Vic were leaving town. I would have gone if I hadn't planned on being here instead of in Virginia."

"It's too bad we have to bother the family on Christmas."

"He'll probably welcome it. He's retiring next year, and this is the kind of arrest that will send him out with a bang. Besides, he's used to getting calls on holidays. Not to mention at all hours of the day and night. It comes with the territory.''

Peggy squinted. "Is that what it's like for you?"

He looked vaguely worried. "You mean, do I get a lot of calls?"

She nodded. "Yeah."

"Is that bad?"

She considered. "Well…no." Pausing, she felt her chest constrict. For the past day or so, as the end of their time together neared, exchanges such as this were creeping into their conversation more and more. What he was really asking was if Peggy could handle the lifestyle of a law enforcement officer. "I just wondered."

"Yeah," he said. "I get a lot of calls. When a case is breaking, I sometimes don't make it home. And right now, I travel a lot. Go to other crime scenes around the country."

Guilt assaulted her. "But you took time off work to look for me."

He seemed to know what she was thinking. "The job's important," he returned, "and there's a lot of pressure to produce results…"

"Do you feel that if you're not working, a life may be lost?"

"Sometimes," he said, appreciating her understanding. "But that's exactly why you learn your own personal life has to be just as important. Agents who can't put themselves first, who feel hyper-responsible and always have to be at the center of the action, always wind up burning out. Or they get divorced. Or they don't have good relationships with their kids. I've seen it happen more times than I can count.

"That was the first thing Ohringer taught me on the job. In the end, people who don't take care of their own lives first do everybody a disservice. They're good agents, but only in the short term. They don't stay in it for the long haul."

She digested that. She was beginning to think Oliver really was as he seemed, a man with staying power. But would that extend from the professional into the personal? "He sounds like a smart guy, this Ohringer."

"One of the best. And a good family man, too."

She started to ask if that's what Oliver wanted, a family, but she didn't need to. His respect for how his boss had handled the pressures of the job was in his voice. He, too, wanted to balance the personal and professional.

"I mean it," she said, shifting the subject and scooting closer to Oliver on the couch, her voice still throaty from their lovemaking. "Before you call…I want you to agree to let me be on the plane."

Blowing out a sigh, he leaned back. Resting his neck on the couch cushions, he rolled his head, sending her a long sideways glance, the heat in it making her feel she was wearing something much more risqué than the blue silk robe he'd gotten her for Christmas. "Once Ohringer's involved, it's not going to be up to me."

"I know, but he'll listen to your recommendation."

"Honestly, I don't think it's such a good idea, Peg."

"I know you sometimes use civilians."

"Only when absolutely necessary."

"Despite how persuasive I've been?"

Smiling, he glided an arm around her waist and hauled her onto his lap. Chuckling softly despite their argument, she snuggled when he spread his legs so that her backside could fall between them, then she hooked her knees over one of his legs. She felt cradled by him, even more so as he circled both arms around her. For a moment, she fell silent, enjoying the solid warmth of his body and the heat from the fire he'd built. He was wearing a pair of gray sweatpants, and as she stroked a hand across his bare chest, stopping to absently twirl dark curls between her fingers, she felt the smooth, worn fabric tease her exposed thigh.

His voice lowered seductively. "You've definitely been persuasive, Peg."

She dropped a nail between his pectorals, drawing an invisible line between them, not stopping until her finger was tracing the drawstring to his pants. "I've loved every minute of it, too," she admitted as he lifted a hand and smoothed her hair back from her face. "Look," she added, "I know you want to protect me, but…"

"I also know you can protect yourself," he said, dropping his hand from her hair and stroking it down her cheek. "You already confronted these people."

"Exactly."

"And now it's time for trained professionals to handle them."

She tilted her head to better survey him, taking in

how firelight flickered in his dark eyes. She'd never seen eyes so intelligent, nor so capable of showing emotion. And yet, there were other times when they seemed to shutter, becoming unreadable. Right now, they were unreadable. "Why did I know you were going to say that?"

His gaze shifted toward the fire, lingering on the white-yellow flames slowly dying to embers. In the bottom of the fireplace, a log had cracked, falling between the andirons, and now the wood chips glowed bloodred like coals. After a moment, he returned his gaze to her. "Why do you want to go?" he said, narrowing his eyes as he took her in.

For a minute, she avoided his gaze. "Because this has to do with me," she finally said, a chill moving through her as she remembered how she'd run from Miles's town house. "I'm the one who got shot at." But of course, it was more. It was pride. Miles had used her in the worst way, making her believe he loved her, when he'd been with another woman. Something about that—about how much pleasure he'd taken in having power over her—made her want to be involved. "I want to see them arrested."

"They'll be arrested. You don't have to be there."

"But I want to be."

"That's the first rule of law enforcement," Oliver schooled. "Never take it personally. The most dangerous thing a person can do is let their emotions get in the way."

Suddenly, her throat felt tight. She wondered if she was the only young woman Miles had used. Given what Oliver had said, there were probably others. "How can you *not* let your emotions get in the way?"

He shrugged. "When bad guys do bad things, it really isn't personal."

It sure felt personal. She thought back to that night at the Rainbow Room, when Miles had proposed. She'd been so excited, so happy; she'd felt her heart would burst from joy. "I think it is," she countered. "Maybe people like that know how to choose an easy mark."

"Bad people will exploit another's weakness," he agreed. "But it's still not personal. People like that are bent on doing harm. It says far more about them than the person who's victimized."

"But I can help you catch him," she protested. She was sure of it. She knew Miles better than the officers did, though she didn't want to tell Oliver. "I was the one who recognized Susan Jones." She took a quick breath, then added, "On the plane."

"Other people will recognize her, too, Peg. While the tape we've made from the phone calls won't be admissible in court, the agents can still use it. From it, we know what disguises they'll be wearing, and that will make them easier to spot."

Lapsing into silence, he smoothed back her hair again, inhaling deeply as he did so, enjoying her scent. "Agents are trained to see through disguises," he continued. "New methods for doing that are always being introduced."

"Like the Quick Composite software?"

He nodded. "Funny," he commented as he

dropped his hand and rubbed circles on her back. "The man's own work will be used against him."

"But, Oliver," she said, picking up the earlier thread, "if the tape can't be used in court, it'll be difficult to show there was an existing relationship between Miles and Susan. He was partially responsible for getting her parole, but even that might be circumstantial. At best, you'll be able to prove that he fudged documents claiming that Susan helped him arrest others by becoming his snitch."

"Rule two of law enforcement," Oliver said. "Our job is to catch the bad guys. Lawyers do the rest."

"I know," she said, still not willing to give up the argument. "But don't you want to establish proof of a relationship?"

"They'll be together on the plane. And we'll recognize them, because she described their disguises during a phone call. Since the tone of the call suggests a personal relationship, agents will start questioning people, canvasing Miles's neighborhood, looking for links between them."

"Such as?"

"Places they might have been seen together. In restaurants. On flights. You weren't the only person who saw them together, Peg, you just happened to be the only one to identify Susan Jones as a fugitive."

"True," Peggy said, even though the couple hadn't really been on the flight. Taking a deep breath, she plunged on. "But wouldn't it be better if something usable established their relationship? They've probably..."

Her chest felt suddenly tight with emotions she

couldn't even name. She no longer cared for Miles. Her feelings had changed the instant she saw him in bed with Susan Jones, but the betrayal still hurt. It was hard to imagine that another person might want to crush her—or anybody else's—hopes, desires or dreams.

Oliver was watching her carefully.

She managed a quick smile. "I was just saying they've probably been intimate for a long time."

"I still say he'll double-cross her."

"Which is why you need a woman."

He smiled. "I definitely need a woman."

She shot him a long look. "I mean on the plane with you."

He turned serious. "What are you proposing, exactly?"

"Well…you say he likes power," she returned, encouraged by Oliver's interest. "And that he would enjoy playing two women off each other."

"That's how his profile stacks up."

"What if I got him into the plane's bathroom with me and—"

"Whoa," said Oliver.

"Let me finish," she volleyed, unable to hide the catch of excitement in her voice. "What could be more tempting?" she asked, talking as the plan began to form more fully in her own mind, "than if Miles had an opportunity to two-time Susan Jones on the plane?"

He arched an eyebrow. "You're going to proposition him? Ask if he wants to have a tryst in the lav?"

She nodded. "Why not? I could wear a wire, get him to talk. According to your profile, it could work."

"Now *my* words are being used against me."

At that, she couldn't help but smile sweetly. "You said he'd like having two women fight over him, right?"

"You want to fight with Susan Jones?"

"Of course not. But he'd want me to. If a sexy flight attendant suggested they have a fling right under her nose, he'd be half hoping his girlfriend would find out…"

"You don't think he'd recognize you?"

She considered, her heart missing a beat. "No. Because I'd be in disguise."

"He's trained to recognize people in disguise."

"You'd help disguise me," she retorted. "Besides, he only…" She took another deep breath. "He only saw me briefly…in the airport parking lot." Now she knew she couldn't tell him about Miles. If Oliver was aware of her history with the man, he definitely wouldn't let her try this.

And should she? She sobered, thinking about the danger of what she was suggesting. "He'll be tense on the flight," she murmured, her mind still working, continuing to form a plan. "He'll be afraid of getting caught. I mean, no matter how grandiose he feels, how powerful, he'll know he's traveling with a fugitive, and that as soon as the plane touches down he's got to pick up money from a bank heist. It's risky. I bet he'll be sweating bullets."

"Maybe. But he sent the money through FBI channels, using his know-how and credentials to get out of the country.''

''Of course,'' she countered. ''But deep down, he's scared. He knows what he's doing is wrong.''

''You think he has a conscience? I'm not sure he does.''

''I am.'' Her blood quickened as she and Oliver hashed this out; it was much more exciting than reading a good mystery, or watching *To Catch A Thief.* ''Think about it. His sixth sense must have told him to look at the items on your desk.''

''For all we know, he looked at the other desks, too,'' returned Oliver, playing devil's advocate.

''Maybe. But what's made him nervous is seeing the paper on your desk with his name on it.''

''Whatever paper he was referring to, it wasn't related to this,'' Oliver assured. ''It probably concerned the Quick Composite software.''

''That doesn't matter. All I'm saying is that, deep down, we've rattled his cage. He's too powerful and in control to show it on the surface, but he half expects to get caught. Whether he looked at your desk, or other peoples', the fact remains that he was scouting around for something suspicious.''

Suddenly, she realized that Oliver was grinning at her. Knitting her eyebrows, she said, ''What?''

A soft chuckle sounded. ''You're good at this, Peg.''

''This?''

''Profiling.''

Suddenly, she laughed, too, and it felt good. For just a second, the tension left her. Probably, it was the realization that she and Oliver shared an interest; she'd like being involved in his work, his cases. "I wasn't lying when I said I was a crime buff."

"And to think I went to school to learn profiling." The sexy tilt of his lips lifted a notch. "Do you know what I'm thinking right now?"

"Oh, I can guess."

"That easy, huh?"

"When it comes to some things, you're predictable," she admitted, her blood quickening now, not with excitement about the case, but because of his touch.

"Maybe I'd have been a better public servant if I'd just read more mysteries," he murmured.

"We'll never know."

They eyed each other a long moment, and she felt an emotional connection in the gaze that she'd never shared with another man. The truth was, she'd begun to think men and women didn't really share such things at all, that this sort of connection was a myth. Only when Midnight leaped onto the couch and curled against his thigh did Oliver break the gaze. Still, neither of them spoke. Sadness suddenly twisted inside her. Whether she was on the plane tomorrow or not, this really might be their last night together.

She followed his gaze to the fire, aware of how its warmth radiated outward, and of the soft sounds it made, of spitting and crackling. Then she took in the light dancing across his cheeks. "It's so homey," she couldn't help but say. There was a curled cat, a lighted tree, a fire in the hearth. And Oliver.

His gaze settled on her again. "What else are you thinking?"

She cuddled closer. "Lots of things." But she returned to their argument. "A woman has the best chance of getting Miles to talk."

Oliver chewed his lip thoughtfully. "You're right. We can send in a female agent. Brief her, so she'll look like an attendant."

"Being a flight attendant isn't as easy as it looks," she countered. "I know that sounds funny," she continued defensively, "but a trained observer might notice if an attendant seems out of place. Besides, as you said, Miles might well recognize one of your own. He'd be less likely to recognize me in disguise," she added, even though she wasn't quite so sure about that.

Dragging a hand through his hair, he blew out a long breath. "You'd wear a wire?" Before she could respond, he cursed softly, then hugged her closer. "Peg, the woman shot at you. As it is, you're lucky to be alive…" His voice trailed off as he brushed his lips across the top of her head, kissing the strands of her hair. He added in a whisper, "*I'm* lucky."

Lifting her chin, she gazed into his eyes. "I know you're concerned, Oliver, but I feel this is right. I'm the one who can help catch him and give you more evidence to make the convictions stick."

He reached past her for the phone. "I'd better call before it gets any later. Ohringer's going to need time to arrange for French authorities to meet us on the ground."

"Us? Does that mean you think I should go?"

As he lifted the phone, he said, "What you've said makes sense. Miles might recognize an agent, although I think I can disguise myself well enough that he won't. You, he only saw once, and briefly, and not in a personal context." Oliver blew out another sigh. "With agents watching, and given the fact that airport security's tight, Miles and Susan won't have weapons, so you need not be in any real danger...

"Okay," he suddenly decided, his eyes meeting hers as Ohringer's phone began to ring. "I'll try to sell the boss on it. I think you've got a sixth sense about this one."

WHERE WAS OLIVER?

Peggy's eyes darted down the long aisle, past Miles and Susan, but Oliver's seat was still vacant. She glanced at her watch. They were only moments from landing in Paris. Ohringer had flown ahead, to help organize French authorities on the ground. Because of Miles's ties with the agency, and because he'd traveled widely, Ohringer feared he might recognize agents on board. But he'd let Oliver travel. In his disguise, he was unrecognizable—blond, blue-eyed, wearing glasses and using crutches.

But where had he gone? To the bathroom in coach? Pressing a shaking hand to her chest, Peggy touched the tiny microphone taped to her skin. A wire ran between her breasts to her belly, then wrapped around her waist, attaching to a voice-activated recording device at the base of her spine.

Exhaling a quavering breath, she hoped it was working. But she could swear Miles was staring at her. In the brown wig and mustache, he didn't look at all like the man she'd dated. No more than Oliver was recognizable. Or herself. She fought the urge to touch her wig. It was white-blond, the thick hair straight, and reaching just past her shoulders. Heavy bangs fell into her eyes, brushing the frames of stylish eyeglasses. Contacts turned her eyes hazel and cheek pads, which weren't as uncomfortable as she'd anticipated, changed the contours of her face. In a mirror, she'd never have recognized herself. Realizing she was holding her breath, she slowly exhaled. Surely, this feeling that Miles was watching her was only her imagination...

Should she make her move now and proposition him? She'd intended to do so hours ago. But no time had seemed right.

That, or she was just too scared. Yes, she was scared spitless. Literally. She licked her lips against their dryness, wondering what had made her decide to play Miss Marple. What if she never saw her mom and Aunt Jill again?

Her heart squeezed, and her eyes stung as tears pushed against her eyelids. If the people who loved her could see her now, they'd be beside themselves—wringing their hands with worry. Oliver hadn't wanted her to do this. Her heart constricted further. When he'd explained that reading true-crime novels couldn't prepare her for real action, he'd looked so worried that she'd been convinced he cared.

And he was right. Being a crime hobbyist didn't mean you could defend yourself in a real crisis situation. She'd learned that the moment Susan Jones had rolled over in bed and shot at her.

Susan Jones.

The woman was sitting next to Miles. Peggy knew neither could have boarded with a weapon, but she was still worried.

And yet she had to go through with this. Only she knew the truth. She was the only one who could get Miles to talk, because she'd been engaged to him. When she considered what Oliver might overhear on the tape, she cringed.

But maybe it didn't matter any longer. Miles and Susan were felons. They belonged in jail. And Peggy had the best chance of getting a confession. Miles devalued women so much that when he talked to Peggy, he wouldn't edit what he said.

Meantime, if Oliver knew the whole truth, he'd never have let her come aboard. But where was he? she wondered again. Miles was continuing to stare at her as if he could see through her disguise. It was unsettling! She watched as he whispered something to Susan, who didn't seem to notice anything amiss.

Peggy's heart hammered as he stood. Had he said he was going to the bathroom? She inhaled sharply. Right now, she was standing in front of the door, blocking it. Unless, of course, he went the other way, to the bathroom in coach.

But no. He was moving toward her. Sweat beaded on her upper lip as she glanced between the first-class seats and the cockpit. On impulse, she pulled the curtain, to shield the first-class passengers from her and Miles's exchange.

Through a crack in the curtain, she continued looking for Oliver. What if she started talking to Miles and Oliver wasn't listening? She smoothed her damp palms against her navy uniform skirt as Miles got closer. "Peggy," she whispered. "Calm down. Just do what you're supposed to do."

This was her big chance to give Miles McLaughlin what he deserved. Maybe her only chance.

A ding sounded, indicating that passengers should return to their seats, but Miles ignored it. Reaching behind her, she twisted the knob on the lavatory door, cracking it open. She'd lure him inside for more privacy. If a passenger interrupted, she might not get the confession.

Mentally, she rehearsed her lines, imagining taunting him. She'd say, "Hey, Miles. I bet you didn't even recognize me. I've been wearing a disguise ever since that nasty trick you pulled, putting my picture on TV. Did you really think you'd get away with that?" Yes, she thought. *Forget the plan you made with Oliver. Don't bother to pretend to be an attendant he doesn't know, who wants to seduce him. Go for broke. Use Oliver's profile. Challenge the man's ego.*

He was only two feet away now.

Then one.

"Hey, Miles," she began, staring at the man she barely recognized in the mustache and brown wig. "I bet you didn't even recog—"

Knuckles hit her solar plexus, lifting her off her feet and knocking her straight backward. She landed on the commode, grasping for her chest, feeling sure the wire had been dislodged. Struggling, she tried to stand, but Miles ground his heel into the toe of her shoe.

"Stop!" she managed. "What are you—"

His hand closing around her throat, he jerked her upward. Pressed against him, she gagged. The door had shut, locked behind him. He was ripping a length of tape from a roll that appeared from nowhere. He looped the tape around her wrists, binding them.

"What are you doing?" she gasped hoarsely.

"Did you really think I wouldn't recognize you?" he snarled.

OLIVER LEANED against a wall near the lavatories in the coach section. It was quieter here. Near the seat he'd vacated, a baby had been crying. He shook his head in annoyance. He'd wanted to keep Peggy in sight, but he couldn't hear over the baby's crying. Besides, she'd shut the curtain up front.

He jiggled the metal receiver in his ear, but something was wrong. Had the mike gotten dislodged? He could swear he'd heard Miles talking.

What was happening? he wondered. Was Peggy sweating? Had perspiration bled into the transmitter? The words were breaking up. "...you thought I was so...so great, didn't...the big cop groupie...and wouldn't..."

Oliver cursed. This was maddening! He never should have let Peggy talk him into using her as bait, but how could he deny a woman who'd so completely stolen his heart? Yeah, she'd done that, he realized, not that he could do anything about it now. He only knew he didn't want to live without her, no more than he wanted to leave her alone with a maniac.

Feeling torn, he tapped the earpiece again. After a moment, he heard humming. A chill went down his back. In a low, taunting tone, Miles was singing the old Buddy Holly song "Peggy Sue."

When the man spoke, the words were still garbled. "...wouldn't get...bed with me. Wouldn't put... out...would you, Peggy?"

Peggy's voice sounded scratchy, as if her throat was raw. "Did that threaten your male pride?"

There was a staticky pause. "...was just using you..."

"Using me when you gave me an engagement ring?"

"Fake. I guess you never had that diamond appraised."

Oliver's eyes widened. What was going on? The mike was clearer now. But he couldn't believe what he was hearing. Miles and Peggy had been engaged?

Everything she'd told him was a lie! Probably, she hadn't seen Miles and Susan on a flight, but had been in some more intimate setting at the time. Suddenly everything clicked—all the bits and pieces that hadn't previously added up. He'd known attempted murder wasn't Susan Jones's M.O. Jealousy, however, might have prompted such an attempt. As surely as when he'd chased Cameron through the streets of New York, he wondered what was truth, what was fiction. One thing was certain. For Peggy, this was personal, and he'd let his emotions get in the way, so he hadn't figured it out. Something that could further endanger her now. He shook his head, knowing he never should have slept with a woman who'd turned to him for help.

Furious with himself, he tried to tamp down the anger flooding him. His whole body tensed while he waited for someone to speak again. Once more, he uttered an oath under his breath. The sound coming through his earpiece was still incoherent.

"It's a good thing I didn't…no sex with…" That was Peggy again.

Oliver guessed that meant she hadn't slept with Miles, and relief filled him to overflowing. Not that he'd care. If she had, it was only because she'd been taken in by a man who prided himself on hurting women. Narcissistic types were users. Even professionals, trained to catch liars, couldn't see through them. But why had Peggy lied to *him?*

Suddenly, her voice came through. "You were sleeping with Susan Jones, remember?" she said. "And what about the database? Did you really attach my picture to her rap sheet?"

Miles actually laughed. "Yeah. Smart of me, huh?"

"Great," Oliver whispered, still reeling from the realization that Peggy and Miles knew each other. Miles had just admitted he'd tampered with FBI files. But Oliver couldn't stand having Peggy trapped in a confined space with such a lowlife. Only years of training kept him from going down the aisle and pulling Peggy out.

That, and the fact that he wanted more of a confession. The French authorities were waiting, and Susan and Miles would be arrested. The aircraft was descending.

"C'mon," Oliver murmured. "Say something."

Another moment passed, then, "…the woman who tried to kill me. Susan Jones. The woman who's sitting out there in 17B. Does she know you're in here with me, Miles?" Peggy was taunting him again. "Aren't you afraid she'll try to kill me again?"

Kill me.

The words seemed to sound from inside a vacuum. The thought chilled Oliver. No wonder she'd looked so haunted and bedraggled that night in the Washington Square Hotel.

The mike turned to static.

Then, "I was scared when I went to your house—" Peggy's voice broke off, and Oliver's heart wrenched when he realized it wasn't from the faulty mike, but emotion. She'd cared for Miles, probably deeply. His profiling instincts told him that's why she'd withheld the information from him; she was that ashamed of being duped. Now she was risking herself to make things right.

"Damn her pride," Oliver whispered, respecting her for it even as he spoke.

"We dated three months," she said. "And… when…found you in bed with a criminal…"

Miles's words were clear. "You hated seeing Susan and I together?"

Miles was obviously loving every minute of this. His voice became even easier to understand. "Is that the reason you're on board, Peggy? At first, I thought you were covering for one of your roommates, and disguised because you're really on suspension. I just figured you needed the money. But now…" His voice was lost a moment, then returned. "I see you're here because you want me back…"

The man's ego knew no bounds.

She gasped. "Here…because I want you arrested. You saw Susan try to kill me!"

"Sure I did," he said. Three unbearable seconds passed. Then Miles's voice cut in again. "…didn't want you…thought you'd come in handy because you worked for the airlines."

"Handy…for when you took off with Susan Jones and all the money she stole in her last heist?"

"That's right."

That was the full confession! Peggy had got it! Oliver was only seconds away from her. Just as he set aside the crutches that were part of his disguise and started running down the aisle, a woman stepped in front of him, blocking his way. Through the earpiece, he heard Peggy gasp. She said, "What's that?"

"A knife."

"You can't have it on board!"

"That's the thing about being a lawman, Peggy Sue. You learn how to break laws." And then softly, in a way that chilled Oliver's blood, Miles began singing the Buddy Holly tune again.

The next thing Oliver heard was Peggy's scream.

12

EVERYTHING WAS HAPPENING too fast! Miles was facing her, blocking the doorway, waving the knife. How had he gotten it through security? Ice was in Peggy's veins. Did Susan Jones know she was in here? Was she going to torture Peggy, too?

Veering from the blade, Peggy swung her bound hands over Miles's shoulder, hoping the punch would push open the door behind him, but the door was locked! Lifting her leg, she aimed for Miles's groin. *Do something!* her mind shrieked.

He shifted away, a smile curling his lips as if he was enjoying this. "So that's how Peggy Sue wants to play." He laughed. "Well, Miles wants to play, too."

The blade glinted, sharp and lethal, under the fluorescent light. Suddenly, the plane dipped, and when it bounced in the turbulence, Miles swayed. The blade was going to slice her jaw! She stayed steady on her feet, though. She dodged the weapon. She'd been flying for years. She feinted left then right, ducking beneath his arm, trying to escape. His fist caught her cold. Bile rose, acidic, burning against the raw lining of her throat. Did he really mean to kill her? Was he that insane? Didn't he know he'd get caught?

Or were Oliver's theories right? Was Miles so grandiose in his own eyes that he believed he could get away with this? As raw terror welled inside her, the plane dipped again, and she heard the whir of metal as the landing gear lowered.

Where was Oliver? Had Miles done something to Oliver before he'd come into the lav? Was Oliver out there, maybe stabbed, lying near his seat? Her heart wrenched. Poor Oliver! She couldn't lose him.

"'I love you—'" Miles singsonged. "'Peggy Sue.'"

Even now he was mocking her for caring about him. As the plane hit the runway, the impact flung them against the washbasin, then Miles brought the blade closer, so the tip nicked her cheek.

She'd always prayed for a safe landing. This time, more than ever, she voiced a silent appeal. Her breath stilled. Casting her eyes downward, she could see the silver glint in the periphery of her vision—so close to her eye. As Miles tilted the blade, it pierced skin. A pinprick of blood popped from the wound.

"Please..." she whispered.

And then Oliver came from nowhere. The flimsy white door was flung back and he filled the frame like a giant. Seemingly, he ripped the door from its hinges. And then he stared inside, his dark, narrowed eyes assessing behind the glasses that were part of his disguise, his eyebrows knitted so tightly that they formed a thunderous ledge.

A large hand thrust out, and Peggy watched in shocked fascination as long, slender, artistic fingers that had touched her so often in sumptuous, exquisite passion closed over the back of Miles's sports coat. With seeming effortlessness, Oliver simply lifted the man and tossed him aside as if he were a worthless piece of debris.

Then, with his voice sounding low and comforting, just the way it did when they were naked in bed and wrapped in each other's arms, Oliver said, "Did he hurt you, Peg?"

With her eyes fixed on his, she became aware that, rather than heading for the gate, the plane had halted. The hatch near the cockpit had opened, and she could hear carts on the tarmac outside. Sharp, staccato French voices filled the air as men swarmed on board. Footsteps pounded.

"It's Ohringer," said a man behind Oliver who grabbed Miles.

"Are you hurt?" Oliver repeated.

He was staring into her eyes as if he feared she was in shock. Maybe she was. Feeling oddly unsure about how she felt now that the danger was past, she reached a finger to her cheek, touched the pinprick of blood, then withdrew the finger and looked at it. "Not badly," she said.

"Damn," he muttered, suddenly stepping forward and reaching for her bound hands, only now noticing them. Leaning, he tore his teeth into the tape, ripping it. As soon as her hands were free, they circled his neck and drew him close.

"Let me go!" a woman—no doubt, Susan Jones— shouted. Vaguely, Peggy realized someone was reading Miles his Miranda rights. They'd find the money easily enough, since it had been transported through

FBI channels. But it didn't matter now. Her arms were wreathed around Oliver's neck, and his mouth was descending. It was firm and yet soft. As warm as a blanket. As life-affirming as a new morning.

She kissed him back.

And for just that moment, Peggy tried to tell herself it wasn't a kiss goodbye.

ON THE GROUND, things were chaotic. The authorities, unsure of what to expect, had summoned ambulances and fire trucks, and passengers were being routed onto buses, which would take them inside the terminal.

As they deplaned, Oliver looped his arm around Peggy's waist, and something about the easy way she moved against him made his heart ache. They fit together so well, each stride said that, but she was going to leave him. He was sure of it. He sent her a sideways glance as they hit the tarmac, deciding not to ask for explanations yet. He wanted her to know that her lying about Miles wasn't their main issue—at least not for him. He was too sure he knew why she'd done it. He was a profiler, after all. "You're going to have to stop at the medic unit."

"I'm fine."

Judging from the glazed shock in her eyes, he doubted it. "They need to look at you."

"I know. I don't mind. I'll get on one of the buses."

Up ahead, he could see a group of French cops surveying him while they talked to Ohringer, waiting for him to near. They'd want to question Peggy inside the terminal, but since he was with the bureau, he'd be stuck here for hours. When one of the men waved, he merely nodded, then he stopped and turned toward Peggy. "Wait a second," he said.

She frowned. "What's wrong?"

Nothing, he thought. *Everything.* The truth was, he wasn't sure. Not yet. Would she continue their affair? He reached a hand around her neck, briefly cupping it before he dislodged the pins that held her wig in place. Lifting off the wig, he stuffed it into the pocket of his overcoat, then simply said, "I want to see your hair."

The truth was, he was looking at each inch of her as if he'd never see her again. Gently, he threaded his fingers through the strands, hardly expecting the sharp, sudden pain that cut through him. Their time was over, and that left him as cold as the French night.

Beyond her shoulder, he could see the lights of Paris twinkling in the darkness, as if beckoning them. Fluffing her hair, he let the locks fall in front as they often did, obscuring one of her eyes. She really did look like a film star from the 1940s.

Cameron, he thought.

She was definitely a dream woman. Feisty, fun and as lovingly homespun as a yarn rug. "Here," he murmured, suddenly realizing she hadn't fastened the open sides of her coat. He glided his fingers over the buttons. "Your coat's not buttoned."

"I have things at Anna's," she suddenly said, apparently thinking the same thoughts as he. What were they going to do now that she could return home?

Were they going to stay in Paris? Return to New York together? Go to Anna's?

He figured the decision was up to her. She knew what he wanted. Her, her—and her. When she'd spoken, her voice had sounded so raw that he'd winced. Now he stroked her neck. He could see where the other man had hurt her, trying to strangle her. "You did good." He really admired the way she'd handled herself.

"Well," she corrected, looking brave as she shivered.

He glided his hands around her waist, bringing her close enough to feel his breath on her lips. Gazing down, he took in her hot, lush mouth…a mouth that had been so welcoming. He found himself thinking of how she'd looked one night, down on her knees, her pink tongue sliding luxuriously along the most intimate part of him. A shuddering breath came from between his lips. "Where were you really, when she fired the shot?"

She inhaled sharply. "In his bedroom. I found them in bed together." In a few sentences, she told him about the relationship.

"Why did you lie to me?" he murmured. "Why didn't you tell me about Miles?"

He could see her throat working as she swallowed, and something about the fast tick of the beating pulse he saw beneath her ear felt like a warning. "It was just a white lie, Oliver," she defended. "The important thing is that he's been arrested now. So has Susan Jones."

Oliver searched his mind. Hadn't they had this conversation before? Suddenly it came to him. When she'd left Anna's apartment to shop, she'd asked him, "Would I lie?"

And he'd said yes.

Then she'd said, "Only little white lies."

He said the same thing now that he'd said then. "No lies are little."

"I'm sorry," she whispered.

"Relationships are built on trust," he said. But she didn't trust him.

"At first, I felt too embarrassed to tell you. And then, I knew if I told you last night, that you wouldn't agree to let me get on the plane and wear a wire."

She was right about that. "It was too risky." If he'd known she and Miles had been intimate, he would have guessed Miles might see through Peggy's disguise and recognize her.

"But it turned out all right in the end, Oliver."

"Did it?" While she had good reasons not to trust men, among them a man named Miles McLaughlin, the bottom line was that she didn't trust *him*. Not exactly the fairy-tale ending, from his point of view.

"They've been arrested."

But that wasn't the end he was thinking about. He was thinking about him and her. She'd said she was sorry. Now he said, "I'm sorry, too, Peg."

He became conscious of a car horn sounding, then a megaphone. Authorities were trying to clear the tarmac so the plane could progress to the gate. "You," a French police officer called to him. "You are from the FBI?"

Oliver forced his eyes from Peggy's, which in the

starless night looked as dark and deep as an ocean. "Yeah."

"She needs to go to the medic," the man called in a thickly accented voice.

"Right," murmured Peggy.

Just as he turned to her again, Peggy quickly reached on her toes and captured his mouth in a sweet, soulful kiss. Their lips locked—perfectly, briefly.

And then she was gone.

She'd turned away fast enough that the hem of Anna's navy pea coat caught the wind and swirled around her thighs. It seemed impossible, but as she headed toward one of the buses that would take her to the medic station, snow began to fall. Or not snow, really. Just flurries.

Tiny pinpoints of white circled around her, making her look strangely surreal, and suddenly Oliver felt as if his heart was going to break. This was too damn much like *Casablanca,* a movie Anna had made him watch more times than Oliver could count. That's what happened to a guy when he had a persistent matchmaking little sister. Right now, Peggy looked like Ingrid Bergman just before she got on the plane.

His body tensed. Should he run after her? He wanted to. He *had* to. And yet there was one thing about which Peggy had never lied—her intention to leave. She didn't trust her instincts. She didn't trust men. Or him. And as a psychological profiler, he knew such a relationship couldn't work, that she had to be ready.

Or at least willing to try.

He imagined himself running after her, anyway, stopping in front of her and pulling her into his arms. She was walking so quickly, though, with her head down, clutching the collar of the coat against a wind strong enough to lift her hair. The strands waved in the breeze.

Oliver guessed that was how she wanted to say goodbye.

"HERE," said Kiki, who was happily playing hostess three days later. She entered the living room carrying a bamboo tray loaded with sodas. "I brought some extra napkins."

"I put all the food on one tray," clarified Sophie, who was on Kiki's heels. "I hope that's okay. We've got eggplant in garlic sauce. Moo-shoo chicken. Stir-fry prawns and more egg rolls than people."

"Not to mention fortune cookies," Isabella chimed in. She tossed a pile of wax packages on the floor along with soy sauce.

Juliette sighed as she seated herself on the floor in front of the TV. "We should have guests more often," she said, glancing around the room and looking pleased. "I never knew our apartment could be so cozy."

Despite her low mood, Peggy couldn't help but smile. "Oh, it's cozy, all right." After she'd left Oliver on the tarmac in Paris, she'd gotten on the next plane back to the States. Just as they'd landed, LaGuardia and J.F.K. had closed due to inclement weather. Now, because of the snowstorm raging outside, all five women were in the apartment at the same time, which was a first.

And, of course, they had houseguests.

"You must have been scared to death during the ordeal," said Aunt Jill who was curled at one end of the couch. *The ordeal* was the phrase Aunt Jill and Peggy's mother had settled on to describe what had happened to Peggy.

"We came as soon as possible," added her mother.

Aunt Jill glanced between her needlepoint, Peggy and the TV news. "Well, at first, when Kay Hill said she saw you on the tube, on *To Catch A Thief,* identified as a criminal, your mother and I just laughed," Aunt Jill said conversationally. "But then, when Mavis Roebuck and Alyssa Evans from church said the same thing, we started to worry. I mean, we didn't *believe* you could do anything wrong, but…"

"Some *man* could have coerced you," explained her mother.

"And one did," put in Aunt Jill.

"That horrible Miles McLaughlin," agreed her mother with a shudder.

"Men," said Aunt Jill simply.

Seated on the couch between her mother and Aunt Jill, Peggy felt her heart swell. She'd been shocked to find them here upon her return from Paris; it was so sweet of them to come. As she glanced from one woman to the other, she was struck by the family resemblance. Although they were roughly twenty-five years older than she, the two other women still wore their hair as Peggy did, and each had inherited the same recalcitrant lock that fell over an eye. Her mom and Aunt Jill, of course, were no longer natural blondes.

But they were hers. And they loved her. Briefly shutting her eyes, Peggy took a deep breath, feeling glad for her personal good fortune. She was safe and sound. Loved. And Oliver…

Fortunately, a male news anchor spoke, cutting off her thoughts. "We're taking you now to New York where Kate Olsen is with a man she's interviewed many times, Oliver Vargo."

"Wait, wait," said Aunt Jill hurriedly. "Here it is! The report!"

Kate Olsen came on-screen. "I'm here right now, live in New York with Oliver Vargo, the bestselling author of *How Evil Thinks* and *Catching Crooks the Old-Fashioned Way*. He's the man who single-handedly arrested bank robber Susan Jones, and her accomplice, FBI agent Miles McLaughlin."

"Not single-handedly," Oliver corrected.

Peggy half listened as he went into her contributions, and assured the public that most agents, unlike Miles, lived on the straight and narrow. Fortunately, he left out her relationship with Miles, although he mentioned that the ex-agent had arranged for Peggy to be identified as a felon on *To Catch A Thief*. It was a crime for which Miles would be charged.

"Also among the charges," said Kate, "is the attempted murder of Peggy Fox, the woman who so admirably helped agents get a full confession from the defendants.

"Ms. Fox, previously on suspension," continued Kate, "is back in good standing with her airline."

The publicity garnered by her heroics had actually brought a pay hike, but Peggy wasn't sure she'd stay. As far as employment was concerned, she'd often had other aspirations. She also kept envisioning Oliver's book covers—and the picture of his house. It was so big, with plenty of room for her and kids.

Her picture came on-screen, drawing her from her thoughts again. It was the same one that had first identified her to Oliver as Cameron, and that had been flashed on the crime show.

"You look so pretty, honey," murmured her mother proudly.

Peggy would have smiled, since the truth was, she looked exactly like her mom, but tears were filling her eyes and she didn't trust herself to speak. She missed Oliver so much.

Things only worsened when Kiki said, "Oliver Vargo—he's not bad-looking, either, eh?"

"Try major hunk," corrected Isabella.

"There's no way you didn't sleep with him, Peggy," interjected Sophie. "Not when you two were cooped up during a snowstorm for so many days. And not when you're already such a big fan of his books. You always had a crush on him."

"He's a law officer," Peggy defended. "He wouldn't sleep with someone he was trying to help."

Yes, she'd told her roommates that nothing had happened. *White lies,* she thought now. *Just little white lies.*

And she could hear him say the words. *"No lies are little."*

He was right, too. She'd slept with him every night.

And what they'd done between the sheets had been every bit as hot as the snow outside had been cold.

Now she still slept with him—in her dreams. All she had to do was shut her eyes, and Oliver's warm, velvet tongue was exploring each inch of her. Right now, she could feel each erect inch of him pressing into her, feeling so blessedly warm, so astonishingly right.

Funny, she thought. She'd entered his life as a dream. She'd been a sex goddess named Cameron whom Oliver wasn't even sure truly existed. She'd become real for him, though, fulfilling every fantasy. Meantime, Oliver, who'd been real all along, had become nothing more than a phantom to Peggy, a man who loved her only in her dreams.

She sighed heavily, snapping back to attention when she heard his name. "Oliver Vargo," announced Kate Olsen for the audience, "a real hero."

"And Peggy Fox," he added quickly before they cut to the studio, "a real heroine."

He'd mentioned her name. Somehow, that fact reminded her that he was still in New York, just a couple of blocks away. Soon, he'd be headed home to Quantico. He'd be gone for good…

"How sweet of him to mention you!" enthused her mother. "And you girls are right. He *is* good-looking."

"And talented," approved Aunt Jill. "He writes books. And from the way he just talked about you, I think he likes you, Peggy."

Maybe Oliver had even loved her. Why had she left him at the airport like that? Was she really so afraid to try with a man? How hard could it be to get hurt again?

"Have you talked to him since *the ordeal?*" asked her mother.

"She said no," responded Kiki.

Nobody seemed to notice she was on the verge of tears. Each time she blinked them back, Peggy became that much more certain they were about to roll down her cheeks.

"Here you go, Peggy!" said Isabella brightly as she slid a loaded plate onto Peggy's lap and tossed her a napkin. "Chopsticks or a fork?"

"Chopsticks," her mother answered for her. "My daughter lives dangerously."

"I thought you'd be afraid for me," Peggy said dryly, reaching past the chopsticks for a fork.

"We would have been," returned her mom, giving her a quick hug, "but we didn't know a thing until *the ordeal* was all over."

"Thank heavens," put in Aunt Jill, patting Peggy's leg.

When Peggy glanced down at the hand that lingered on her knee, her heart seemed to twist inside her chest. Probably, she shouldn't be wearing the bathrobe Oliver gave her for Christmas. Just looking at it seemed to transport her back in time. Suddenly, she and Oliver were lying on the water bed again. She was floating, rocking with the waves, while his lips were in her hair...then on her cheeks...then drifting down to her breasts. As he licked the tips, she shuddered with more pleasure than she'd ever thought possible...

"Aren't you going to eat, honey?" asked her mother.

"Ever since *the ordeal*," said Aunt Jill worriedly, "she hasn't been eating much."

"I'm starved," Peggy assured.

But before touching her dinner, she opened a waxy white packet and took out a fortune cookie. Snapping the cookie in two, she slipped out the fortune.

It said, *Don't lie to yourself about love.*

Epilogue

"OLLIE, will you please tell me what's wrong?" Anna's voice came over his cell phone, sounding staticky.

"Nothing."

He was peering through the trees, wondering if he'd really heard a car door slam. All he saw was the Irish setter puppy he'd picked up at the pound yesterday. The dog was racing in circles around the yard's only dogwood. Most of the trees were sycamores, oaks and ashes, and the branches were heavy now, drooping under the weight of snow and icicles. Still, there were enough evergreens to obscure the road from Oliver's vision. Because his property was isolated, people got lost out here all the time.

"Ollie? Are you listening to me?"

"Huh?"

"See?" said Anna. "There's definitely something wrong, Big Brother. According to what you're telling me, you're sitting outside in a hammock in thirty-degree weather."

"I've got a chair, too," he defended. It was the one *she'd* gotten him for Christmas.

This only seemed to further annoy his sister. "It's snowing," she huffed. "Vic and I are coming to

Quantico right now. We'll spend the night with you and ring in the new year."

"You have plans. A big party, remember?"

"I know." Anna sounded torn. "But I'm worried about you."

Glancing around, Oliver decided that Anna was probably right to worry. He did look odd, sitting in a hammock in the snow. So what if he looked weird, though? Who was looking? He'd been reading the *Sex Files*, which he'd brought from Anna's apartment, and sipping cocoa from the plastic mug to his thermos. He'd decided to get a head start on midnight. "Don't worry," he said. "I plan to give myself a big kiss."

"Vic and I are packing right now," Anna vowed. "Should we pick up anything on our way?"

"This may not be the best night for you and Vic."

Anna sounded hurt. "It's that woman, isn't it?" she guessed. "The one you thought was Cameron?"

He didn't see any reason to lie. "Yep. Sure is."

"Vic and I are coming," she said again. "We can be there in just a few hours, Big Brother."

"Not tonight."

"But it's New Year's!"

Maybe. The last thing Oliver needed was a newly engaged couple in his home. No, he didn't want to see any of it—not the kissing. Or the meaningful, private glances charged with significance. He definitely did not want to awaken in the night to hear squeaking mattress springs or giggles. If he had to watch people French-kissing as the clock chimed midnight, he was sure he'd go over the edge.

"Why don't you call her?" urged Anna.

"Because you're on the phone?"

"If we hang up, will you call?"

No. "Maybe."

"Oliver—" She groaned. "You're older than I am, and I'm already engaged."

"So?"

"So, I think the oldest child should get married first," Anna returned. "That's the way it's supposed to be." She suddenly gasped. "Oh, Ollie, I'm sorry, but I have to go. Vic's due home any minute, and I promised I'd have something ready for dinner." She sighed. "Look. You think about all this, and if we're allowed to visit, Big Brother, then you call me back in fifteen minutes. Okay? We care more about you than the party we're supposed to go to."

Oliver tried not to recall how domestic he'd gotten with Peggy, and how good it had felt. "You?" he teased, ignoring that she'd invited herself and Vic again. "Cooking?"

There was a long stunned pause, then Anna said, "Uh...no. I'm calling the Indian place around the corner. They deliver, and I can't call while we're on the phone. Probably, I should get conference calling, so I can make two calls at the same time, but..."

Her voice trailed off and Oliver couldn't help but laugh, but as soon as he'd said goodbye, clicked the phone's off-button, and shoved the instrument into the back pocket of his jeans, he felt strangely bereft. Talking to his sister, no matter how in love she sounded, was better than talking to no one at all.

At least day after tomorrow, he got to go back to

work. Susan's and Miles's arrests had shaken things up, so there'd be more than the average paperwork to keep him busy. Especially since the ridiculous policies Miles had initiated for producing a paperless FBI were now being rescinded. Kevin Hall had been promoted, which was good. As it turned out, he'd been suspicious of Miles all along. Kevin had only gotten close to Miles to document Miles's more questionable office practices, something that would help make all the convictions stick.

Sighing, Oliver flipped up the collar of his wool coat, then turned the pages of the *Sex Files* again, pausing when a picture of Cameron fell out. Before he'd returned to Quantico, Anna had insisted on crossing the Quick Composite software with the Sex File statistics once more. She and Vic were hoping the FBI would formally allow them to do so for next year's *Sex Files* publication.

He took in the picture. This time, of course, the woman looked nothing like Peggy Fox.

The woman Quick Composite produced was a surprisingly toothsome, girl-next-door brunette who brought Sandra Bullock to mind. The text, of course, had remained the same. A smile played over Oliver's lips and he shook his head as he read it again. *When she has to get dressed at all, Cameron likes to get out and have spicy, erotic adventures. She especially loves the excitement of world travel and meeting new male playmates.*

His eyes skipped downward. *Exploring kinky aphrodisiacs is her favorite pastime, and she dabbles in everything from body paints to edible undies. Cam-*

eron will do absolutely anything—and everything—to please her man.

She'd definitely done that.

Glancing up, he looked around for the puppy.

That's when he saw her.

She was standing in front of a snow-frosted evergreen, about thirty paces away, wearing a long red coat he'd never seen before and a matching red tam. She was wearing a skirt, too. He could tell because the hem was fluttering an inch below the coat, just meeting a pair of knee-high boots. Dressed in red, with the evergreen behind her, she looked the very picture of Christmas. The Irish setter he hadn't yet named was running circles around Peggy, dodging inward to sniff her feet, then whirling away. A bottle of bubbly dangled from her hand.

Oliver didn't move. He couldn't. And if the truth be told, for a moment, just as during those haunting November days a while back, he doubted his sanity. One too many times, he'd chased this woman's apparition through Manhattan streets, and now he couldn't quite believe Peggy Fox was really here.

Resting the *Sex Files* on his chest, he nodded toward the tree behind her and lifted his voice. ''I thought angels went on top of the tree.''

During the pause that followed, he found himself doubting his sanity once more. Was he starting to go buggy, out here alone in the woods? After all, he *had* spiked his cocoa liberally with whisky, preparing for a very lonely New Year's.

''Some angels walk on the ground.''

''Prove it,'' he said, but his heart swelled in his

chest at the sound of her voice. She sure sounded real. "I want to see footprints."

Slowly, Peggy began walking toward him, the light winter breeze lifting her hair, reminding him of the way her hair had looked at the airport, the strands waving as if in goodbye.

Was she saying hello now?

He gazed where her black, lace-up boots were leaving prints in the snow. She'd certainly left prints in his life and on his heart. "You're no apparition," he decided, sitting up as she reached him. "Have a seat," he added, nodding toward the chair she'd gotten him for Christmas.

She nodded her acknowledgment but didn't sit. Instead, she leaned, set the champagne bottle in the snow, twisting it so the snow served as an ice bucket, then she snagged the paper from his lap and took in Cameron's picture, chuckling softly. "She doesn't look like me at all."

"No. You're prettier than Cameron."

She glanced at him. And that's all it took. Just one look. Their eyes locked, and worlds passed between them. There was hunger, hope, vulnerability, sexual need. Reaching, he grasped her hand and pulled her into his lap. He bit back a gasp as the hammock rocked beneath their weight, and was astonished at the thrill that moved through him. His groin tightened at her touch; his skin warmed. He wanted—no, needed—to take her mouth and plunder it, but… "Why'd you come back, Peg?"

"For you."

"Right now, you're America's Sexiest Woman,"

he returned, his breath ragged as he leaned backward, lying lengthwise in the hammock and urging her on top of him.

"Kiss me," she whispered as his fingers pushed into her hair, knocking off the red tam. "Forgive me for running away," she continued as it tumbled to the ground, into the snow, resting beside the champagne. "I was scared."

Before his lips caught hers, he whispered, "You're not now?"

"Sure," she said between kisses that were turning more languid. "But not so scared that I don't want to be with you."

"Good," he murmured before his mouth found hers again. "We can ring in the new year and maybe name my new best friend."

"I thought *I* was your new best friend."

"You are." He could only stare into her face, and he could barely believe his eyes. She was so breathtaking. Her flushed cheeks were the color of roses and as soft as velvet. It was hard to believe she wasn't a figment of his imagination. But the next kiss was very definitely real. Hot and deep, it turned needy for both of them.

His hand slipped between them. Unbuttoning their coats, he opened them. "This way," he murmured in explanation, "we can stay wrapped in each other and use both coats for blankets."

"Sounds cozy, Oliver."

He nodded, his heart thudding in his chest as he felt their hips lock. The mound of her pelvis found him, crushing him where he was becoming aroused.

As his hands circled her back, he drew in a sharp breath that brought her scent to his lungs. Insistently, against the zipper of his jeans, he started throbbing, and the sensation was so intense it was nearly painful.

"I've missed you," she panted.

There would be a long time, he figured, to talk in depth about their relationship. Right now, the important thing was that she'd walked back into his arms. And his bed. Or at least his hammock. He slanted his mouth across hers once more, deepening the kiss when he felt her nipples harden against his chest. "I can do something about your missing me," he assured huskily.

She was smiling, and he suspected that the extra glimmer he saw in her eyes was from unshed tears. "That's why I came for New Year's," she said. "So, you could do just that, Oliver."

He didn't need any coaxing. Just seeing her across the yard had gotten him so wound up he wanted to explode. Gasping, he glided his hands downward, curving them over the fleshy rise of her backside. Flexing his fingers, he drew her to him, arching as he did so.

"Let's go inside, Oliver."

"I don't want to waste that much time."

She laughed in delight. "Uh…I think we'd better. I wouldn't want your…" She paused delicately. "Your…you know, to freeze and fall off. If you know what I mean."

"As hot as I feel?" He chuckled as his hands rustled her skirt upward, so he could explore the tights she wore beneath. "Not a chance, sweetheart."

As he dived a hand between her legs, he emitted a soft moan. She was hot to the touch. And so damp that she'd soaked the hosiery and panties. Twisting the fabric, he tugged, testing it, then he suddenly yanked, ripping it. By the time she realized he'd torn a hole, it was too late for her to protest.

Not that she would have. "What an animal," she whispered, sounding pleased.

He couldn't help but laugh, despite how badly he wanted her. "When we went up to Anna's roof on Christmas Eve, I told you I was saving the lions, tigers and bears for last."

She said, "Show me."

One more hard tug left her tights and panties in shreds. Another brought down his zipper. Easing his jeans and briefs down on his hips, he urged her to straddle his thighs. Neither realized they were outside. Or in thirty-degree weather. The warmth inside their coats and embrace was too kinetic, the friction they created too hotly joyous.

They were almost there—panting, riding, laughing together with the sheer pleasure of what they were doing—when his dark eyes turned serious. "Promise me," he murmured.

"Anything, Ollie."

"No more lies."

She shook her head.

"And you'll never vanish again?"

"Never," Peggy whispered, the sexual moment deepening to completion as she glided an inch farther down on his hard, waiting shaft. Shuddering, she slid all the way down, the dizzying descent slow and sizzling...until he touched her womb, and their bones met, and the space between them vanished and they were truly one.

"Never," she whispered then. "Never, ever, again, Oliver."

HARLEQUIN® *Blaze*™

From:	**Erin Thatcher**
To:	**Samantha Tyler;**
	Tess Norton
Subject:	**Men To Do**

Men To do!

Ladies, I'm talking about a hot fling with the type of man no girl in her right mind would settle down with. You know, a man to *do* before we say "I do." What do you think? Couldn't we use an uncomplicated sexfest? Why let men corner the market on fun when we girls have the same urges and needs? I've already picked mine out....

$ Saving Money $ Has Never Been This Easy!

Just fill out and send in this form from any October, November and December 2002 books and we will send you a coupon booklet worth a total savings of $20.00 off future purchases of Harlequin and Silhouette books in 2003.

Yes! It's that easy!

I accept your incredible offer!
Please send me a coupon booklet:

_____
Name (PLEASE PRINT)

_____
Address   Apt. #

_____
City   State/Prov.   Zip/Postal Code

In a typical month, how many Harlequin and Silhouette novels do you read?

❏ 0-2   ❏ 3+

097KJKDNC7   097KJKDNDP

Please send this form to:

In the U.S.: Harlequin Books, P.O. Box 9071, Buffalo, NY 14269-9071
In Canada: Harlequin Books, P.O. Box 609, Fort Erie, Ontario L2A 5X3

Allow 4-6 weeks for delivery. Limit one coupon booklet per household. Must be postmarked no later than January 15, 2003.

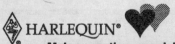